Praise for *Th.*

"Castro's debut novel uses the process of writing (and not-writing) to reflect on social media's inescapable and numbing pull. It also upends the historical 'drug novel' by offering a portrait of what life looks like in recovery. The narrator's hopeful reorientation out of this simulated, technological world opens space to be present, to think of his partner, and to return home humbled by the machinations of the actual world."

—Taylor Lewandowski, *Bookforum*

"*The Novelist*'s observations about using social media . . . are accurate, but where the novel really exceeds the standard criticism is in turning this distraction into the drumbeat of modern life, on top of which a compelling guy riffs about life, literature, and pooping . . . Castro has an ear for comic timing and eye for the kind of observations that linger just below consciousness."

—Hanson O'Haver, *Gawker*

"Castro's fiction debut is as meta as it gets, but that's part of its immense charm . . . Sweet, funny and beautifully written."   —Michael Schaub, NPR, a Best Book of the Year

"Very funny . . . [A] critique of his, and our, collectively frayed attention."

—Maddie Crum, *Vulture*

"Our terminal obsession with modern day distraction is crystallised in Jordan Castro's debut novel, titled *The Novelist* . . . A prescient, witty book." —Douglas Greenwood, *i-D*

"Jordan Castro's *The Novelist* nails the experience of being online, in all its abject glory."

—Kate Knibbs, *WIRED*

"Jordan Castro's debut novel, *The Novelist*, cleverly cops to its influences—like Nicholson Baker's early reverential mundanity yoked with Thomas Bernhard's righteous wit—but brings a philosophical fervor to its charismatic self-indulgence . . . It's a careful report on the mental gymnastics so familiar to our tech-addled brains, a roast of the stunted evolution of small press literature, and an earnest metafictional brooding over what a novel should do. Its titular narrator practically pleads, 'I wanted my first novel to be taken seriously.' *The Novelist* deserves at least as much."

—Crow Jonah Norlander,
Los Angeles Review of Books

"Compact, brilliant, and very funny . . . Castro has committed the unlikely act of attending to his art while *including* its corruption, a tradition all its own, thus making it all the more contemporary and comedic."

—Scott Cheshire, *The Brooklyn Rail*

"This book, better than any other I know, shows how creation emerges from the nothingness of our culture. A hilarious and important novel."

—Michael W. Clune, author of *Gamelife* and *White Out: The Secret Life of Heroin*

"Brisk and shockingly witty, exuberantly scatological as well as deeply wise, *The Novelist* is a delight. Jordan Castro is a rare new talent: an author highly attuned to the traditions he is working within while also offering a refreshingly fun send-up of life beset by the endless scroll."

—Mary South, author of *You Will Never Be Forgotten*

"Jordan Castro brilliantly manipulates time and perception in *The Novelist: A Novel*. Prescient, funny, and deeply uncanny, this is a wholly unique book about distractions, digressions, and what it means to make art and live meaningfully while trapped in the bright, narcotic thrall of social media." —Kimberly King Parsons, author of *Black Light*

"I admire the ingenious invention of *The Novelist*, in which an unnamed writer struggles to write his book, begins to write another book, and ultimately writes this book, which is blunt, earnest, self-critical, provocative, philosophical, and very fun to read." —Kathryn Scanlan, author of *The Dominant Animal*

The Novelist'

The Novelist

—— a novel ——

Jordan Castro

Soft Skull
New York

First Soft Skull edition: 2022
First paperback edition: 2023

The Library of Congress has cataloged the hardcover edition as follows:
Names: Castro, Jordan, author.
Title: The novelist : a novel / Jordan Castro.
Description: First Soft Skull edition. | New York : Soft Skull, 2022.
Identifiers: LCCN 2021044746 | ISBN 9781593767136 (hardcover) | ISBN 9781593767143 (ebook)
Subjects: LCGFT: Stream of consciousness fiction. | Novels.
Classification: LCC PS3603.A8877 N68 2022 | DDC 813/.6—dc23/eng/20211005
LC record available at https://lccn.loc.gov/2021044746

Paperback ISBN: 978-1-59376-725-9

Cover design by www.houseofthought.io
Book design by Wah-Ming Chang

Published by Soft Skull Press
New York, NY
www.softskull.com

Printed in the United States of America
1 3 5 7 9 10 8 6 4 2

For Nicolette

The Novelist

¶ opened my laptop, still waiting for my morning tea to steep, and tried to type my password three times rapidly before getting it right, my waking fingers clacking with the determination of a machine. The high-definition snowy mountaintop and valley full of trees appeared in front of me; "[Fri] 8:14 a.m." in the upper right-hand corner; 94 percent battery icon beside it. I touched my face, adjusted my position on my wooden chair. The sun peeked through the cheap venetian blinds, closed and hanging over the window in front of me, my small black kitchen table pushed up flush against the wall. I focused my eyes and touched the trackpad on my laptop with my middle finger, then dragged the cursor on the screen toward the bottom row of icons, and, inhaling deeply, I clicked.

The internet opened and I immediately clicked the Gmail icon—which appeared on my homepage next to my other "Favorites" in a row across the top of the screen: Facebook, Twitter, a link to a picture of the "less than" and "greater than" symbols that I'd accidentally saved there (I'd wanted to get a tattoo of the sideways caret symbol on my pinky finger, such that from other people's perspectives it would signify "greater than," but from mine it would signify "less than")—and not Google Docs, where the novel I'd been working on was saved.

I vaguely sensed, during the one or two seconds it took my Gmail inbox to load, that I was doing something I did not want to do, but I experienced this hazy awareness as so far from any predominant consciousness that acting on it wasn't even a possibility, whatever recognition of dissonance it created immediately rendered, passively, to a class of feeling like that of "sitting on a small fold in one's pants" or "registering a barely perceptible noise in the distance." I hated checking my email first thing in the morning. It set a bad tone for the rest of the day.

Three unopened emails confronted me—one from Li, one from my boss, and an alert that my

Jordan Castro novel had shipped; I mistakenly thought I saw one from Eric, causing my heart to flit—which I clicked and scanned quickly. My boss's required no response; I glanced at the shipping alert, which I'd clicked only so it would no longer appear as unread in my inbox.

I clicked Li's email last. "Having my morning poop now / via iPhone," it read.

I adjusted my position on my chair, rather pleased, then moved the cursor into the reply box and pressed down on the trackpad. Before settling at my kitchen table, before preparing my now-steeping tea, I'd spent two minutes on the toilet, and it occurred to me that Li and I had probably been pooping at the same time. I was delighted. I typed "we must've been pooping at the same time," then clicked Send.

A flush of blood, or something, I felt, rushed into my brain; a small but notable spike in my mood; then, without the slightest hesitation—besides the second or so it took me to move the cursor from the send button at the bottom of the screen to the + button at the top—I opened a new tab and clicked Twitter.

I had specifically not wanted to click Twitter before working on my novel. Every morning, I woke with the general intention of not clicking Twitter, and, with varying degrees of effort and success, I resisted until I half-convinced myself of a legitimate reason to click Twitter, or, in a weak moment, clicked it unthinkingly. Sometimes, I weakly justified or rationalized: I didn't have very much to do that day; I wanted to check up on [current event]; I would only click once, then not click anymore . . . On the morning in question, however, I attributed my reckless willingness to click to a subconscious desire to prolong the unexpected rush of having fired off a spontaneous email to Li. My body wanted another surprise; but I also wanted to work on my novel.

Twitter, over time, had proven calamitous when it came to getting work done. I clicked unthinkingly, often feverishly, and if I started in the morning, I would generally continue, unhinged, throughout the day, on both my laptop and my phone, everywhere I went, no matter what else I was doing. Through trial and error, I'd observed that if I refrained from clicking Twitter in the morning, I wouldn't check it so much throughout the rest of the day, and so I turned this into a kind of rule: Don't check Twitter before noon. But this—self-knowledge and the imposition of a

rule—didn't do me any good; the clicking continued more or less unabated, and once it began, it
was out of my hands. The more I clicked Twitter,
the more I wanted to click Twitter, and so on.

I watched as it loaded in front of me.

White header, matte blue background, tweets
against a white background, two columns, various sections. There was a second or so after the
general layout loaded that the notifications hadn't
yet appeared—a moment when the notifications
button was visible, but the number of notifications was not—and I felt a microburst of yearn-
ing as I waited. This was an intentional feature
of Twitter, I'd learned from a podcast, which I
recalled abstractly as I sat there—this slightly
delayed gratification, coupled with the varied re-
ward of the number of notifications, activated the
same area in one's brain as a slot machine—while
feeling dimly aware of my having immediately
done something I specifically hadn't wanted to
do to start the day.

The notifications button finally displayed the
number—one. Fffff, I thought.

I clicked.

I had gained a new follower. I moved my cursor in the direction of my new follower's username

and avatar, hovering over it briefly, noting how many users they followed (1,338) and how many followed them (687). My new follower's username and avatar entered my mind semiconsciously as a collection of letters and numbers, accompanied by a dark image; the username contained the number 37, with letters around it. There was something about my new follower that felt bad; I intuitively disliked them. I moved the cursor away from my new follower without clicking their profile, and clicked back to Twitter's homepage.

The cursor, independently of me, it seemed, though my finger was indeed moving on the trackpad, inched toward the notification button again just after landing on the homepage. I wanted to work on my novel. What was I doing? There were many benefits of not checking one's followers, I reminded myself. For one, it would increase the time I spent working on my novel. But the main benefit was that if anyone ever asked me why I didn't follow them back, I could say honestly that I hadn't seen that they'd followed me. This was a problem I'd mostly encountered in high school: people in hallways or classes accosting me, disguising their pathetic insecurity with a playful remark, a despicable quip meant to bait me into following them back—*I followed you on Twitter last night*, or *Hey, why didn't you follow me back on Twitter?* or, the most sinister and manipulative of all, *Your tweets are so funny*. After high school, it didn't happen as much, because I didn't see as many people, but it still happened occasionally, mainly at literary events, which are entirely indistinguishable from high school in every relevant way, so I needed to be careful about what I did or didn't do.

I tried to be intentional about the people I followed: I didn't want to be confronted with content from people I didn't like, and I wanted to see every tweet from those I did like. I also wanted to give off the impression that I was well liked for my tweets, that I had not accrued my followers, as so many had, through the weak-willed grift of simply following whoever in hopes that some might follow me back. A helpful way of calculating a person's real follower count was to subtract the number of people they followed from the number who followed them: that was how many followers they had. When I was younger, and Twitter was new, I thought about these things often, and I took them very seriously. I had other thoughts too, but over the years I forgot them. Now, I occasionally rationalized following someone for reasons other than the quality of their tweets—there were more complex reasons to follow someone than tweet quality alone; life was holistic; Twitter did not exist, as it were, in a vacuum, I told myself. However, I did hate Twitter now, possibly because at some point I had begun following too many people on it.

So I resisted the urge to click the notifications button again. My new follower was simply not worth it; I felt a surprising amount of contempt for whoever it was.

Now, on Twitter's homepage, I scrolled: "everyone wearing fanny packs this year would have ridiculed anyone wearing a fanny pack five years ago - you all are horrible"; a picture of a clothed chest with an "I Voted" sticker on it; "Dance for joy! Coffee mate seasonal flavors are back!" with a GIF of a cartoon coffee cup dancing next to a giant Coffee mate creamer bottle; a blurb for a forthcoming novel; "i can't believe food costs money"; "Ayyy is just short for amen."; "I've seen the word 'neckbeard' used to refer to antithetical things."

I grinned. I slid two fingers forcefully upward on the trackpad, then held them there, the heel of my hand anchored to the base of the laptop; tweets scrolled by, blurred, like one mass of text, until everything stopped—I really did not want to be looking at Twitter.

I tried to think of something but couldn't remember what I was trying to think of. Perhaps I hadn't wanted to think of anything specifically. I visualized getting up, going to the bedroom, picking up *The Mezzanine* by Nicholson Baker off the bedside table—was it on the bedside table?— then walking to my reading chair, sitting in my reading chair, and reading it. Reading a novel might help me refocus the morning.

My novel, I recalled with trepidation. My novel was what I'd been trying to think of, and why I had wanted to focus in the first place. My novel, which had been making me feel dejected and unwell, due to its badness, was the opposite of *The Mezzanine*. My novel was not cerebral or immaculate, like *The Mezzanine*, and, due to its having been written in the third person present tense, by me, had no texture or insight at all. I would begin work on my novel now, I resolved. Perhaps I could try to channel *The Mezzanine*. I began moving the cursor around Twitter's homepage in an aimless, vaguely circular manner, flinging my pointer and middle fingers in small, twitch-like spurts, and watching the cursor flail on the screen, like a fly against a window. I stalled for a few seconds this way, scanning but not reading tweets, then clicked Gmail, then Twitter again, in less than one second.

I scrolled Twitter and saw tweets about Donald Trump, retweets from accounts I didn't recognize, and one tweet that included the word "hot." My back and jaw clenched as I passively registered the barrage of awful content; I didn't so much process the tweets as absorb the tone and length of them. I felt increasingly like I was staring at the screen from a face that was not my actual face, but was somehow behind or inside of my face—my "second face"; like I was inhabiting an auxiliary body inside of my body; my outer body was the actor, operating independently of me—"I" was somewhere inside of myself, behind my outer face, my "skin face"; there was no conscious sensation in my hands.

I considered the fact that my skin face was attached to my fingers, then formulated the thought in a questioning tone—My face is . . . attached . . . to my fingers?—as I fragmented still further, becoming confused by the concept of skin and the meaning of the word "attached," all while feeling physically numb and continuing to scroll absently, in quick spurts.

I scrolled past a tweet from Li. I scrolled past three tweets from Eric. I scrolled past tweets from writers who I only knew online. I scrolled past a tweet from Violet. I scrolled past two tweets from Jordan Castro.

My vision softened as I scrolled; the screen appeared farther away than it was; the tweets became blurry—I considered my novel abstractedly. My novel was a third person, present tense, short-chaptered account of three days in 2015, during which I was going through severe benzodiazepine and heroin withdrawal in a house where I'd just signed a lease with my soon-to-be-ex-girlfriend, while the people I'd been working for, selling weed, called me constantly about the exorbitant amount of money I had lost in a blackout and now owed them. I had been working on the novel for five months; I'd started it when I moved here to live with Violet in Maryland, where I could now write about my life in Cleveland as something that existed more concretely in the past, and not, as it had felt while I lived there, in one big, hopelessly continuing present.

I abstractedly considered my novel's perspective and tense: the fact that it was in the third person present tense distressed me. It was the perspective and tense I'd begun writing it in, and it was the perspective and tense I felt most comfortable using, but when I imagined myself, anxiously, as a reader who wasn't me reading it, my novel felt lifeless and voiceless and empty and bad—all of which I attributed to the perspective and tense. I had recently looked for other novels in the third person present tense, something to model mine after, but found nothing worthwhile. The only book I'd ever read in the third person present tense was *Chilly Scenes of Winter* by Ann Beattie; I anxiously recalled a friend, in an interview, saying that he "didn't trust" third person writing. Was I writing in the third person because it allowed me to distance myself from the protagonist? Was I writing in the present tense to avoid getting "under the surface of things"? No—it was better not to get under the surface of things. I stared at the screen, my vision still soft, my thoughts soft now too, as if they had followed my eyes, as I sat in front of the screen, completely still, my fingers and the corners of my eyes and mouth microscopically quivering, not quite considering my novel, experiencing myself in a pre-language state, more closely approximating images than words, though occasionally becoming aware of incomplete thoughts like "Third person . . ." and "Fuck."

Wasn't Li's first novel in the third person present tense? And Eric's novel? I snapped out of my trance; it felt like many minutes had passed, though it had probably only been seconds; I opened a new tab, then closed it immediately. I clicked my Twitter username and looked at my own profile.

Fuck, I thought grimly, feeling something approximating despair, or grief. I scrolled a little further down; my Twitter was horrible—Twitter in general was horrible. It was as if at some point in late 2014 someone had unleashed a bug that made everything on Twitter completely horrible. Twitter used to make me laugh, I lamented, but it didn't make me laugh anymore. Once, Twitter had contained nothing but funny, interesting tweets; now Twitter contained only boring and horrible gibberish. I imagined myself as an ogreish monster, clumsily slamming the keyboard with thick, hairy hands.

Doooo, I thought.

When I was younger, I'd viewed Twitter as an art form. The 140-character restriction imposed by the tweet box was, to my young mind, comparable to restrictions imposed by other poetic forms; it was also the only poetic form based on the unit of "character." Twitter, like everything else, I naively surmised, was art.

I remembered this attitude the way one remembers having been touched inappropriately as a child; my skin felt sensitive and cool; Twitter was one of the few things that had given me enjoyment as a teenager; I had really believed it was special and good; now the truth had been revealed to me. Twitter had become a grisly hellscape of parasitic babblers, dominated by the nothing-lords, seeking nothing and creating nothing, destroying and *deconstructing*, complaining and resenting, mindlessly snatching at scraps, and whoever could lord over these nothing-scraps least gracefully gained the most nothingness . . .

Young people believe such silly things, I thought. Young artists and writers, especially. I continued to stare at my Twitter despairingly.

A series of unthinking maneuvers led me to a list of users who had liked my most recent tweet;

I read every name on the list, then scrolled to the top of the list and lingered for a moment before clicking out of it. I scrolled up to the top of my feed and clicked Home. Twitter . . . I thought, abandoning the thought there.

Animals . . . I thought, as if I was attempting to continue my "Twitter . . ." thought but had misfired and gotten "Animals" instead. Ani . . . I clicked the notifications button and looked at my recent likes, retweets, and replies; I became aware of the sensation of my brain operating on more than one level: I sensed that I was clicking things compulsively in a manner that was causing me low-level distress, but I couldn't muster with sufficient force the will required to effect any behavioral change. I considered clicking my new follower's profile, but I did not. Just this past week, I had been followed and unfollowed then refollowed three times by the editor of a low-level literary magazine, the name of which I recognized, although I'd never read an issue. That is exactly the kind of thing I got myself into when I checked my new followers, I considered—I got thrust into some deranged editor's undignified psychodrama; sucked into some vacuous sycophant's bizarre self-worth battle, involving me when I did not want to be involved . . . I moved my hands off the trackpad and onto the table.

I moved my fingers back onto the trackpad and clicked back to Twitter's homepage; I clicked Gmail then Twitter in essentially the same motion, two consecutive clicks, quickly and unthinkingly.

Fuck, I thought, simply.

I considered my novel.

My novel, which so far didn't include any mention of Twitter, was based on a time in my life when I hadn't thought much about Twitter at all. The opening scene was a fictionalized flashback of an afternoon in late 2014, when I was getting ready for a friend's funeral. As I was trying to remember how to tie my tie, the postmaster general called, having intercepted a package for "Dillon," which he said he believed was meant for me, then told me to come to the store where the package was sent. Rattled, I ran around my house in my funeral clothes, destroying burner phones, scales, and other potential evidence, then throwing the remains away in a dumpster before going to meet him. At the store, I declined to answer any of his questions as he pulled many vacuum-sealed pounds of weed out of a box, while my friend, the owner of the store, and the only reason I'd agreed to show up, sat crying in the corner. Six or seven men, some DEA, some Cleveland police, began threatening to confiscate everything in the store if no one claimed the package, so I claimed the package, which seemed to set the officers at ease.

Before I got there, my friend later told me, the officers had learned from googling me and looking at my Facebook and Twitter accounts that I was a writer.

"We know you're a writer," they'd said sympathetically. "And writers don't make that much money. Someone offers you a couple hundred bucks to catch a package here, you think, 'What the hell?' It makes sense, man. Just tell us who paid you to get the package sent here."

I looked away from my laptop, twisting my neck, a kind of stretch, toward the still-steeping tea on the counter. It glowed amber, like beer, in the strands of morning sun that managed to break through the blinds; a few stray tea leaves floated inside the french press: floating there, my little stray tea leaves. I considered getting out of my chair and approaching the tea—preparing a cup to drink—but refrained. I liked to steep the tea for as long as I could stand to not have caffeine in the morning: this way it would be extra potent, having steeped for a long time, made even stronger by my having waited for as long as I could to consume it, thus increasing my physical desire in direct proportion to the actual strength of the tea, creating a tea that was, as a result, twice as strong.

I'd been drinking yerba mate in the mornings because it gave me less anxiety than coffee, which had started to make me feel so stressed after drinking it that I'd often be rendered a paralytic mess, a shivering invalid, not completing anything, tensely mashing random keys on the keyboard, or worse, staring blankly, as if my eyes were frozen in ice. Yerba mate and guayusa—an upper Amazonian cousin of yerba mate—were the only two drinks that gave me the desired effect without the consequent uneasiness. I liked to drink a full french press before Violet woke. To prepare it, I dumped five or six servings of loose-leaf yerba mate into my thirty-two-ounce french press, then poured 175-degree water onto it. I sometimes liked to pour the water against the wall of the glass and not directly onto the leaves, in order to watch the water sweep the tea up and swirl the leaves together energetically, like ants trying to escape heavy rain. While the tea was steeping, I would plunge the screen halfway down and pull it up quickly at varying intervals, to agitate the tea leaves, and to—as my coworker phrased it when he showed me how to brew it at my old job, and as I've thought of it since—"get the stank."

I scooted my chair back using my thighs and butt and stood up.

Stank, I thought, making my way from the kitchen table to the counter. I imagined myself waddling, like a duck, toward the french press, but continued walking normally. I enjoyed these walks toward the counter to plunge; they reminded me of smoke breaks at my old job; in the four seconds it took me to reach the counter, away from the screen, I relaxed.

I tapped my fingers on the countertop gingerly. I had no idea, generally, what things were made of, and had only ever considered the countertop briefly as fake marble? But standing at the countertop, having just tapped my fingers on it, I considered its substance. Granite? No. Fake . . . marble? I touched the countertop again, sliding my hand across it, briefly perceiving myself as a bartender, then shifted my attention toward the tea. My tea, I thought. I gripped the french press by the wooden handle with my left hand and placed my right hand on the plunger; I angled my right arm such that if I needed more strength I could muster it, though I doubted I would need to, as it was currently a simple matter of getting the stank—not fully plunging.

Lifting my elbow in the air at a sort of right angle, I pushed down on the plunger. I pulled the plunger back up then pushed it down again three times. The leaves swirled busily in the golden-brown concoction, then floated down as I pulled the plunger up again.

I considered beginning my caffeine consumption right then, but resisted the urge and walked back to the table and sat. I centered myself in front of my laptop and moved my finger on the trackpad.

The screen lit up!

It's a miracle, I thought, scooting my chair in a bit more, wiggling my torso briefly, like a fish. It's a miracle that things work. A mixture of genuine awe and self-consciousness came over me gradually. I was aware, as I noted the miraculousness of the screen lighting up, that I was to some degree quoting an interview I'd recently read, in which Jordan Castro passionately raved in a crazed manner about how "miraculous" it was that "things worked."

I had felt something like shame while reading the interview, because I'd expected to hate it but found myself agreeing with a large portion of it—journalists often grouped Jordan Castro's name with figures I found utterly disagreeable, and he was often described using highly charged but ultimately meaningless political terms, all of which, I discovered after reading his books and interviews, were based on egregious misrepresentations of things he had said or written, or, more often, had no bearing on his actual views and were simply slurs meant to slander him—until Violet, who had never heard of Jordan Castro, sat down next to me and immediately began agreeing with what he was saying too.

Fuck, I thought, in reference to the passing, fragmented awe I felt about my laptop working. For most of my life I had believed everything was broken. I had believed everything was broken in a manner that, I'd only recently begun to understand, blindly assumed things that weren't true. My whole life I had been oriented toward the world in a manner that reflected me back.

I'd always started with myself, only pretending to look outward, and only pretending to look inward too. I'd always viewed malice and tragedy as the only true facts of my life, ignoring everything else that didn't fit my self-serving narrative. I had believed that everything was broken when in fact the opposite was true: everything worked! Even that which didn't seem to work worked. It's an unbelievable miracle, I thought, parroting Jordan Castro.

I closed Twitter and, again, found myself looking, inadvertently, at Gmail. Li had already responded to my email. "Had multiple long satisfying pleasing poops / via iPhone," it said.

Inhaling and re-centering myself, I resolved to start writing. I would respond to Li later. But first, I wanted tea. I scooted my chair backward, eliciting a small, subtly grating squeak, and walked jauntily toward the counter. I gripped the wooden handle of the french press and plunged the screen down aggressively, to agitate the tea leaves one last time, before pressing it down again slowly, then strongly at the end, to—as I thought in the moment—"milk the stank."

I watched many stray tea leaves ascend through the plunged screen into the now dark-brown liquid, and I recalled my old french press, which was bigger and better than the one I was using, and which I'd broken only a week ago.

My old french press, a glass Bodum with a red plastic exterior, never had this problem: it never let any tea leaves, let alone many tea leaves, escape into the tea. My old french press, the Bodum, was perfect. Each sip from a cup of tea prepared with the Bodum was crisp, clean; containing no malicious, bitter little tea leaves like with this one. Mm, I thought, the Bodum didn't have this problem at all; in fact, it didn't have any problems. It was perfect—far better than this old, seemingly brandless french press. Nothing sticking to your lips, teeth, or gums; nothing ruining each sip with the bitter flavor and bad texture of stray leaves; nothing ascending through the liquid as you milked the stank from the lengthily steeped tea leaves first thing in the morning . . .

Basically, everything went well with the Bodum, whereas nothing went well with this one.

At first I thought I wouldn't care. I'd always had a high tolerance for bad-tasting things as long as they produced the desired effect. I'd even begun, over the course of the week since the Bodum broke, viewing the stray tea leaves as good, because they presumably contained caffeine, thus I would be consuming even more caffeine with them in the cup than without them. I'd always consumed for effect, and I also got used to things quickly, so, standing at the kitchen counter, watching the stray tea leaves float upward and then begin to fall gently—not thinking anything of it, as this was commonplace for me by now—I felt only an excitement to consume.

I loved the feeling of warm liquid moving through me. The first sip unfailingly felt stream-like—rushing across my tongue to the back of my mouth, down my throat into my chest, then pooling, presumably, in my abdominal organs—and I was intrigued by how it seemed to satiate my need for caffeine right away; how it always, impossibly, seemed to perk me up the instant that it touched my mouth. This was something I'd noticed before and had spent many inattentive minutes, driving or daydreaming while working on my novel, considering: caffeine seemed to work impossibly fast; it touched one's tongue and worked at once; in the morning, the first sip of something hot and caffeinated enhanced one's sense of well-being immediately. It reminded me of going through heroin withdrawal. Just holding a tiny bag of heroin caused withdrawal symptoms to abate; simply preparing to do heroin made the sickness go away. It wasn't quite the case that the caffeine withdrawal that accrued overnight was alleviated just by holding a bag of tea; however, the discomfort did seem to magically disappear after the first sip or two, before my body could have possibly absorbed it.

Yerba mate and heroin, I thought stupidly, standing at my kitchen counter. Could I include this insight in my novel? My novel did take place when I was withdrawing from heroin, and I had started drinking yerba mate shortly after that. Another difference between yerba mate and heroin, I considered, half-convinced that I was working on my novel, was that yerba mate created a good feeling that increased gradually with each sip, whereas heroin created a feeling that was as good as it was going to get right away. Yerba mate gradually swelled, whereas heroin gradually waned.

I felt like an idiot. I remembered with embarrassment that, in a recent text message to my boss, I had described the mild euphoria I experienced after drinking a large amount of yerba mate as "like being on a low dose of MDMA," which my boss had rightfully mocked. It was an unfortunate use of language, to compare things that weren't drugs with drugs, even though I'd ultimately concluded that the description had been accurate. (Thinking about this later, while writing, it had occurred to me that there was in fact an excuse for this comparison—caffeine was a drug! It is okay, I'd thought then, with some relief, to acknowledge that certain drugs are similar to other drugs. It was certainly okay to think, "Yerba mate is an ever-elevating swell, while heroin is an ever-descending suck"; it was unquestionably acceptable to notice that "the first few sips of tea in the morning alleviate caffeine cravings impossibly quickly, just like holding a small bag of heroin alleviates some withdrawal symptoms"; and it was not disagreeable at all to text, "The feeling of drinking large amounts of yerba mate is similar to being on a low dose of MDMA.")

In pursuit of this feeling, I shifted my gaze to the cupboard.

I needed a mug.

I raised my left arm and opened the left side of the cupboard, then raised my right arm and opened the right side of the cupboard: there, on the middle shelf, were the mugs. Rather, there were the clean mugs. My options seemed unusually limited: Violet's insanely gigantic mug (which I never drank from), two regular-sized mugs, and a tiny mug that had the text "I LOVE GRANDMA" printed on it, which I'd purchased from a thrift store in a blackout.

I scanned the kitchen for more mugs. In the sink, filled with dirty dishes, were two more of Violet's mugs, both of which she'd stolen from the graduate lounge at her university; however, I noted with mild consternation, my favorite mugs were nowhere to be seen. I reached down and moved some dishes in the sink, inadvertently causing a plate to slide and loudly crash into a stack of bowls and silverware.

There were two mugs I specifically enjoyed drinking from first thing in the morning. One was the Florida mug. The design, both aesthetically and functionally, was flawless. A serene, colorful landscape, featuring clip art–style graphics on the front; baby-blue water graced the bottom of the picture plane, culminating in a wave up the right side of the frame, which led the eye up to a rainbow—red, orange, yellow, green, blue (the same blue as the water)—and back down around again. It was magnificent. Sprouting out of the water, just in front of the left end of the rainbow, were three black palm trees and some brush, all tastefully reflected in the water. Following the internal lines of the palm trees up toward the sky, there emerged two clip art seagulls, circling a red-and-white sailboat, all contained beneath and framed by the rainbow. Printed across the water, my favorite part (besides the functional aspects): the word "FLORIDA" in yellow-and-white-striped block letters.

It could have been the fact that only the top halves of the letters in "FLORIDA" were striped, while the bottom halves were entirely yellow, or it could have been something else entirely, but for some reason the mug struck me as vaguely pornographic.

The only aesthetic flaw of the mug was the all-caps "MADE IN KOREA" printed crookedly in black on the bottom. It made perfect sense for the manufacturer to put it there so the drinker would never be accosted by the sight of it; however, it would not be very pleasing for a third party to observe from across a table or room. Thus, while the Florida mug was aesthetically pleasing, the

"MADE IN KOREA" at the bottom of the mug displayed, in no uncertain terms, that it was a mug designed for the enjoyment of the drinker, with no consideration for whoever may, unfortunately, be sitting in front of the mug while it was used. This was, in part, why I liked to drink from it first thing in the morning—I was alone. It was also a sensuous pleasure to drink from.

The physical makeup of the mug was exquisite. It could hold just over twelve ounces of liquid but was lighter than the standard mug, which I attributed to the thinness of the mug's "walls." This could have been a problem if, like Violet, I were a slow drinker—the beverage would get cold more quickly—but fortunately, I have always been a fast drinker, and thus have been able to enjoy the positive aspects of thinner mugs throughout my life without the downside. Additionally, the curve of the Florida mug's handle seemed to have been made specifically for my long, slender fingers, allowing me to hook my pointer finger through the handle while it rested comfortably atop my middle finger, supported by my ring and pinky fingers, my thumb resting gently atop the sleek, curved handle. A sensuous pleasure, I considered, scanning the kitchen frantically for the mug. Where is my sensuous pleasure? I thought. Fuck—fuck.

The mug was a pleasure to hold and, due to its weight, to lift. The mouth of the mug—the unforgettable mouth of the mug—was curved outward, uniquely, such that there was a slight overhang, a minuscule widening near the top, which aided the liquid in flowing out such that, though the drinker was obviously the one doing the tilting and sipping, the drinker felt helped by the mug. The mug seemed to sweet-talk the liquid out of itself, coaxing the tea to flow smoothly into the drinker's parted lips, onto his or her tongue with a tad more momentum, a bit more pressure, than expected, which had a calming effect: it was as if the tea were asserting itself, telling the drinker, *This is how it is supposed to be.*

This was the mug—my preferred morning mug, the Florida mug—from which I wanted to drink my first cup of yerba mate while I worked on my novel, but it was not in the cupboard or sink. Where was it? I scanned the living room surfaces quickly. My other favorite mug, I recalled unhappily, was on the floor of my car behind the driver's seat, where I had carelessly dropped it after drinking tea while driving; my car was full of empty containers and trash. I tried to visualize the Florida mug in there but couldn't; I reluctantly retrieved one of Violet's mugs from the dish-filled sink, washed it quickly with the sponge and whatever residual soap may have been left on it from its previous use, then placed the mug on the counter, picked up the french press, and poured the yerba mate.

I pursed my lips, inhaling air with the hot tea in a burst of focused sucking, a small sip, the tea touching my tongue but not the roof of my mouth—until I swished it between my cheeks—then disappearing into me; it was a joyous experience; simultaneously new and familiar; I scooted my chair toward the table and adjusted the crotch of my pants; I put the mug down. I was ready to work on my novel.

I picked the mug up and sucked another small sip. The comforting warmth—partly the actual warmth of the tea, partly the "warmth" of the promise of ensuing good feelings—filled me. I savored the sensation as I moved my finger toward the trackpad and dragged it in circles, essentially rubbing the trackpad, and my laptop screen lit up—confronting me with my Gmail inbox, yet again.

I opened a new tab, then, curiously, instead of typing "doc" into the search bar then clicking the suggested hyperlink below titled "shit dream + more — Google Docs," like I'd intended to, I clicked the Facebook icon in my "Favorites."

My morning so far felt beyond my control, like it was happening to me, not because of me. My chest filled with air, which I expelled from my mouth and nose thuddingly. I ran my hand through my hair—I hated Facebook. There was nothing good about it. Facebook had always been miserably pointless and bad; the impossibly ugly concoction of boxes and squares, blues and greys, seemed to taunt me from somewhere inside the screen.

For much of my adolescence, I hadn't had a Facebook. I'd made one, briefly, after many of my peers switched from Myspace to Facebook, but I'd felt uncomfortable and deleted it shortly thereafter. I'd intuited even then that Facebook was something to be regarded with suspicion. The feverish glee with which people began talking about this new *Facebook* put me at once on the defensive, as I sensed that something new had begun to possess my peers, something which seemed fundamentally at odds with my nascent intellectualism, and which was very annoying. In short, I hadn't been one of those make-a-Facebook-right-away types; I hadn't made a Facebook right away.

Myspace, however, Facebook's predecessor, I had liked. It doubled as a music platform, which was what drew me to it initially. Many of the punk bands I liked had had Myspace pages, and, because of the Top 8 function, where users curated their top eight friends and where musicians curated related artists, it was easy to navigate smoothly, finding new punk bands one after another as I went along clicking, listening to new punk music endlessly.

Facebook, on the other hand, initially emerged in the voices of only the most popular people in the hallways of my high school, and it seemed to be something else entirely, though what, I wasn't sure. Indeed, Facebook never became the music platform it had at one time attempted to be. Facebook had had an age limit—users had to be college students in order to make accounts—which meant that only my peers who had older friends or siblings knew about Facebook, and while I'd had older friends, they did not talk about Facebook.

The people I knew in high school with Face-book accounts must have lied about their ages, I considered. I couldn't remember the timeline exactly . . . high school? Was it middle school? I remembered one of my classmates, a conventionally attractive blond named Ashley, telling me that the reason she'd made a Facebook was because it was a good place to store all of her pictures. "It's a good place to store all your pictures," she'd said, smiling, in environmental science class. Sitting at my kitchen table, as I did while sitting in class then, I wondered why she'd had so many pictures. I remembered her too, in that same class, angrily telling me about how another girl, her best friend, had been trying to steal her boyfriend and had given a blow job to one of her exes. "Like, whatever. How big is your biggest?" Ashley had said—I remembered the exact tone in which she'd said it—while holding her hands a length apart, presumably to indicate the size of the biggest penis she'd sucked. I hadn't understood her pride in having sucked a bigger penis than her friend, and it affected me. Was she exaggerating the length with her hands? How big was my penis?

Now, nearly a decade later, sitting at my

kitchen table, I became vaguely aroused, remembering this strange detail about Ashley, a classmate who I had barely known in high school. I understood now why one might feel proud of sucking a large penis, but . . . I typed Ashley's name into the search bar and clicked.

In her profile picture, Ashley stood with two older people, presumably her parents, on a snowy mountaintop near a lake. I clicked the picture, which enlarged it, then hovered over it with the cursor. I clicked the arrow on the right side of the picture, which took me to her previous profile picture: her and a man, arms around each other, smiling, also standing on a mountain. Her husband or boyfriend—the man in the picture— was notably thick; he had a thick neck and a wide face. I clicked rapidly through her other profile pictures, many of which, especially the more recent ones, also contained thick men.

I wondered whether or not Ashley's pictures were in chronological order—she looked the same in all of them, and they all contained similar-looking thick men, or similar-looking female friends. I recalled other times in recent years when I'd searched the names of popular high school classmates—usually one name, after remembering something unexpected, or see-ing someone pop up on my feed, before clicking other profiles from there via tagged pictures or posts—and all of them, based on their photos, looked exactly the same as they had in high school and were constantly surrounded by thick men, or similar-looking friends.

Moving quickly, almost frantically, as though trying to complete an urgent task, I navigated back to Ashley's profile and clicked her header photo: a group of wealthy-looking small women and thick men, all white, wearing dresses and high heels or blazers and partially unbuttoned button-ups, standing crammed together on a roof, a skyline I didn't recognize behind them. I did, however, recognize some of the people in the picture. At least I thought I did—when I moved the cursor over their faces and bodies, the names that appeared were unrecognizable to me.

I could have lived so many lives, I considered abstractedly. Every person in the picture looked exactly like a person I had gone to high school with. I experienced a kind of vertigo; the past met the present uncannily; people I knew in high school became flattened, mashed together with these strangers into a frozen, vacation-themed mass.

I hadn't been on vacation in years, and I became aware of how little my morning resembled a vacation; my shoulders were rounded and my neck was stretched forward; I was definitely not on vacation. Though I'd grown up around many vacation-posters, people like Ashley who, I'd learned from previous Facebook excursions like these, loved going on group vacations and posting pictures of themselves on vacation together, I hadn't become one such vacationer. At times, feeling insecure, I experienced this divergence as violent—the photos seemed to conceal a dark cruelty—and at others I experienced the vacation photos as sad: everyone in the friend group grinned the same sterile grin, eyes wide and slightly unfocused, as if something loomed behind the camera . . .

I surveyed the picture again. Not only did Ashley look the same now as she did back in high school, I thought, but she also *looked exactly the same as everyone else in the picture.* Her new friends looked exactly the same as her old friends, and they all looked the same as one another.

Everyone, with the exception of a few of the men, stood with bent knees. Many of the girls had placed their hands on their knees; the men had their arms around the girls or each other.

Suddenly, as though roused from a deep sleep—or, impossibly, roused from sleep into another sleep—I imagined arguing about racism with one of the thick men in the picture. The existence of people who looked like that baffled me. I never saw people like that in real life anymore, and even when I had seen them in high school, even when we had talked and laughed and gotten along, they had seemed somehow a mythical other to me.

Perhaps it was a matter of thickness, I considered. Much of life likely changed based on the size of one's body; I didn't, after all, end up with any thick friends. I clicked back to Ashley's profile, placed my hand on the trackpad to scroll down, but stopped instantly, confronted with a picture of her at a party with two beet-red men.

The red men held red cups, and most of the buttons on their shirts were unbuttoned. They wore Mardi Gras beads and were making faces evoking Edvard Munch's *The Scream*: one of them had a buzzed head and exposed chest hair beneath a pink polo; the other appeared prepubescent, a blond in a checkered green-and-white button-up beneath a navy sweater with a zipper collar. They both looked frighteningly inebriated;

Ashley, on the other hand, appeared sober and composed.

I scrolled down a little further, past two videos that featured cute animals in the thumbnail and one video by someone called "The Political Cowboy," then came upon a picture of Ashley with her entire friend group from high school. The picture actually looked like it might have been taken in high school; I assumed it was old; but after looking more intently, I could tell that it was recent—some of the women, though appearing identical to their high school selves upon first glance, were, upon closer inspection, slightly bigger.

Feeling like I was somehow breaking the law, while self-consciously perceiving myself as "acting like a school shooter," I examined them, all of the "popular girls" from my high school—their waxy, smiling faces; their heavy makeup—and it occurred to me that, contrary to what I'd always vaguely assumed, it was not their attractiveness that had made them popular in high school, because they were not attractive. It was something else.

Was it a desire for thick men? I considered, half-jokingly. The marrying or dating of thick men? I didn't think so. The thick men were unattractive too. But men, I knew, didn't have to be beautiful. So what was it? Searching, like a detective, I scanned the photograph of the women for clues. Everything—the background, their clothing, even the other shapes on the screen around the image—seemed flattened into an eerie, shiny sameness. Then I understood. They all looked exactly the same as they had looked in high school and they all looked exactly the same as each other—but they also *all looked exactly the same as their mothers.* This was the one thing they all had in common: they looked like miniature versions of their mothers. They had the thing that made young girls look like adults and adults look like young girls: money.

Kelsey looked just like her mother; Rebecca looked just like her mother; Ashley looked just like her mother—and their mothers all looked exactly like them. I had discerned this from previous Facebook excursions: the more a suburban mother looked like her daughter, the more she looked how she wanted to look. If, when one encountered a rich suburban mother and her daughter, one was unable to tell them apart whatsoever;

if, when one looked at a rich suburban mother and her child, they looked like identical twins . . .

I scrolled up and clicked the Facebook icon in the upper left-hand corner of the screen, which brought me back to my news feed. I took a sip of my tea and looked at the upper right-hand corner of the screen: 8:25 a.m.

I felt disturbingly similar to a fish. What a shitty way to start the morning. I narrated my dissatisfaction to myself with a frustrated "Ffff"; I considered deleting my Facebook; I wasn't going to delete my Facebook. I felt powerless. Something in me lurched, slowly rose, like a monster emerging from a marsh; bubbling liquid and gas; fog; I was unable to discern—did I need water? or to poop?—then I realized, rather shocked at its simplicity: I was hungry.

I navigated from Facebook to Gmail; I wanted to work on my novel for a while before I prepared and ate a meal—I didn't want to procrastinate any longer by cooking, or become foggy from digestion—so I reached for the bananas in the wicker basket on the table in front of me, ripped one from the bunch, peeled it, and bit in. Mm. I took a sip of tea then another bite of banana.

The banana was good. As I sat staring vacantly at my inbox, mashing the banana in my mouth, I recalled when an employee at The Market, the small grocery store across the street from my old job at an arts store, where I worked for a while after I was ousted from the weed-selling operation, had verbally accosted me, ruining my lunch break, when he said to me, unprompted, that he could "really taste the difference between organic and inorganic bananas." Though it was a seemingly insignificant interaction, I remembered it vividly, often, when I ate bananas or was deciding which bananas to buy in the store.

"Like, with some fruits it doesn't matter as much," the grocer had told me, apropos of nothing, as I stood there waiting for my sandwich, "but with bananas you can really taste the difference." I had nodded and agreed, mumbling, "Yeah," and averting eye contact by pretending to look at something on my phone; however, in the years that followed, I'd come to ponder this proposition more exactingly: while it was true that one could taste the difference between an organic and an inorganic banana—between any organic and inorganic food, really—I struggled to think of what he could've meant by "with some fruits it doesn't matter as much." Which fruits had he meant? This was the question that haunted me whenever I recalled this wholly unnecessary interaction.

Compared to most fruits, it almost certainly mattered less if a banana was organic or not, because of the inescapable fact of the peel. The part of the banana one ate was protected by a thick skin—the same was true of the grapefruit, orange, pomegranate, pineapple, avocado, melon, lemon, and lime—so the quantity of pesticides consumed per banana compared to a berry or pear, for example, which one bit directly into or ate in its entirety, must be relatively small. The taste difference would surely be reflected in this fact.

I didn't know much about how pesticides were applied, or what other kinds of hormones were involved in the production of inorganic bananas—perhaps there was some kind of injection, or a modification to the seed that affected the whole fruit—but this inauspicious comment from the overeager grocer struck me as simply wrong.

Munching my delicious organic banana, sitting at my kitchen table, I recalled visiting my grandmother in the hospital when she'd had pneumonia, and eating the so-called apple they'd served her with lunch. My grandmother, thirty years off opiates, refused medication for the pain that she was in, and so it hurt too much for her to bite into the apple. But it was just as well. This "food," served by the hospital to my sick grandmother, had tasted like stale water congealed in plastic; a mutated parody of an apple, not an apple; a nominal "apple" far worse and more unappetizing than any apple I'd eaten preceding the hospital visit or since. I recalled too that in high school, my mother had told me about an article she'd read, written by a doctor, which claimed that it "wasn't worth it" to eat inorganic apples, due to how many pesticides remained on the skin, even after rinsing it "in a salad spinner."

The salad spinner bit had stuck with me—the doctor had, I guess, invoked the salad spinner as the apogee of apple cleaning?—and, sitting at my kitchen table, munching my way down to the end of my perfectly ripe, organic banana, I thought about the man at The Market. Why would he have said something like that, so sparkly and un-nerving, and also so very likely wrong, to me?

The peel of my banana had come undone in four neatly equal parts, which pleased me as I peeled it back for what would likely be the final bite: no stringy bits; nothing unusually dispro-portionate. This must be another benefit of its being organic, I passively hypothesized: fewer pesticides meant less struggling with the peel.

With my free hand, I plucked the last bit of banana from where it was couched in the peel, then plopped it into my mouth—a heftier portion than I'd anticipated; I briefly struggled to breathe; moving my jaw as quickly as possible, I swal-lowed a large chunk of banana before putting the peel next to my laptop, chewing then swallowing the rest. I shifted my weight onto my right, then left, buttock a few times; adjusted my genitals and the crotch of my jeans. I navigated on the screen to Google Docs, where I then opened my novel.

The thought of working on my novel excited and distressed me; it felt like there were small, dull bubbles in my stomach, pulsing menacingly; something seemed to be swimming inside me; it was not dissimilar to the feeling I'd had before eating the banana; I imagined the banana in my stomach, whole, before a clarifying thought presented itself to me: I had to poop.

Any time I left my laptop unattended, I made sure to minimize the internet in case Violet walked past and decided to look at my novel, which was highly improbable now, as she was asleep in the bedroom. Regardless, I minimized the internet then walked to the bathroom, making a small detour to discard my banana peel on the way.

Standing on the small rug in front of the toilet, overhead fan humming, light on, I slid my hands into my pockets then stood there, momentarily frozen, caught off guard by the absence of my phone. I needed to poop; I scurried out of the bathroom, back into the kitchen; my phone wasn't there.

Fff, I considered. When had I used it last? I scanned the kitchen quickly. Where was it? I could just poop without it; it would probably be better to just poop without it. I walked back toward the bathroom, this time pausing in front of the bedroom. Aha!

I saw my dog and, momentarily forgetting about Violet, was overcome with the immediate desire to blurt out my favorite nickname for him, which had evolved over years from "buddy" to the unrecognizably related "Chanstado," as I entered the bedroom. Violet lay asleep on her side, Dillon curled in the crook of her knees; he peeked his head up when he heard me come in. "I'm just getting my phone," I whispered.

My phone, an iPhone 5s with a heavily cracked screen, which I hadn't used yet this morning, lay glistening, it seemed, on the bedside table, plugged in. Dillon groaned, emitting his classic asthmatic grunt-sigh combination, then put his head back down to sleep; Violet made a noise and put the back of her right hand against her forehead, looking, I thought then, Victorian.

"Hiiii," I whispered, crawling onto the bed.

"Mm," Violet said, shifting beneath the covers. She lifted her hand and sleepily waved me away. This also struck me as Victorian, and oddly attractive. I kissed her several times on the forehead and arm. "Mm, mm, mhm." She rolled over, away from me, pulling the comforter up around her neck; I kissed her face again, then stripped the covers off her upper body and kissed up her entire arm.

"I love you," I said, hovering over her.

"Mmmm," she pleaded breathily. She looked

beautiful. She shooed me away again then pulled the blankets back up tight around her.

Dillon lay elongated, tail wagging, staring up at me. "Hi buddy," I whispered. "My sweet boy." Dillon wiggled his whole bottom half when I spoke; I rubbed his head and torso vigorously.

"Mm," Violet said, annoyed.

I looked at Dillon. "Sweet boy," I said with finality, patting him once more and winking. I shimmied backward off the bed, pecking Violet once more as I did. I unplugged my phone and went into the bathroom.

I pulled my pants and underwear down around my knees while lifting up my T-shirt and sitting on the toilet; thunderous gas escaped me. My back and neck slumped; I pulled my phone out of my pocket, pressed the circle button at the bottom, tapped my password in quickly—my birthday— then opened Instagram.

The first post I encountered was a video of my friend Maggie's dog pulling something out from behind an oven then eating it. I scrolled and saw a picture of a manatee; a picture of some candles and food on a table; a picture of a writer I knew and her daughters; an advertisement for the website AthleanX.com.

Unlike with Twitter and Facebook, I didn't struggle with a near-constant desire to delete Instagram, even though I checked it just as frequently. I felt much less troubled by it; I actually kind of liked it. Pictures, though niggling at times, weren't as nauseating as text; the captions and comments on Instagram were auxiliary, and, much of the time, I didn't read them. Twitter and Facebook had devolved into a kind of text-based theater, with people showing only the worst parts of themselves, hurling half-formed opinions and immediate reactions at one another, while Instagram remained a space where people still attempted something less aggressively debasing; where people shared pictures from their lives, attempting candor, or—though they most often failed at this miserably and had no understanding of what it meant whatsoever—beauty.

In practice, Instagram did not produce beauty, or candor, and lent itself only to a different kind of lie. In short, Instagram was vanity and Twitter was pride. Twitter would kill everyone then kill itself; whereas Instagram would only peter out, slowly disappearing into a kind of pleading void.

Of course, there were also those troglodytes—probably the same ones who dominated

Twitter—who were just as ugly, in every sense of the word, on Instagram as they were on Twitter, posting pictures of their disproportionate bodies, videos of their rants and sad music, or, the most repellent recent development, text boxes—attempting to *subvert* and *empower*, or worse, *make a statement*, but the nice thing about Instagram was that this could be avoided. On Twitter, I saw content not only from the people I followed, but also from accounts the people I followed replied to, liked, and retweeted; there were "recommended" tweets and "promoted" tweets—advertisements—all essentially conspiring to assault me with content, in hopes that I might spend more time on the site and interact with as many accounts as possible. On Instagram, I was not unconsentingly thrust into seeing variously indecent posts from accounts I didn't follow; I only saw posts from those I followed, save for some ads, unless I chose to explore.

Sitting on the toilet, I exited Instagram, having only been on it for five or so seconds, and then immediately reopened it. I scrolled, swiping up with my thumb and tapping gently on the screen to stop the scroll at each picture: the face of a writer who I'd never met; an ominous Japanese-seeming structure; a friend's painting; a plate containing baked beans, white bread, eggs, and what appeared to be breaded fish. I double-clicked the circle button at the bottom of my phone and swiped repeatedly up, exiting Instagram, as well as all the other apps that had been open: Safari, Twitter, iMessage, Apple Music, and Gmail. I tapped the Safari icon—a blue circle containing many tiny white lines, which alternated in length, and a half-red, half-white diagonal needle, like a compass—which brought me to the internet on my phone, which looked different than on my laptop. Here, there were two rows of icons: the top, unlabeled, containing links to the Apple website and the Bing, Google, and Yahoo! search engines; the bottom contained FREQUENTLY VISITED websites—Twitter and Facebook.

I tapped Twitter, then double-clicked the circle button at the bottom of my phone and swiped up, exiting everything. I instantly reopened the internet and tapped Facebook. I tapped the notifications button and, seeing no new notifications, double-clicked the circle button at the bottom of my phone and swiped up. My behavior barely entered my consciousness; I was like a mouse in a laboratory, reacting to stimuli.

I tapped Instagram.

Often I sat on the toilet for minutes before anything budged, no matter how badly I'd originally felt I needed to go, looking at things on my phone. There seemed to be a physical threshold that, once passed, poop could flow freely from, or through, but until then I was condemned to lightly strain while trying to pass the first in what would hopefully be a series of many satisfying bowel movements. I'd gone to the bathroom earlier, but hadn't truly been successful: as with writing my novel, I often needed caffeine to get it done.

If I strained too hard, something might "pop" or "break," I intuited, a fear not based on experience, but born of my imagination, though I didn't doubt its possibility; so this morning I strained just enough to feel tension, not too hard or for too long—looking up and to the right, face scrunched in a concentrated scowl, at a blue towel in my periphery, hanging, before relaxing my strained muscles and returning my now-focused eyes to my phone.

I scrolled past a picture that a poet from New York had posted, of a skeleton holding a can of beer and a cigarette, with the text "let's do tomorrow?" below it; a picture of a friend of a friend from Cleveland, a photographer, wearing a sun hat behind a pale-blue rope fence, with the caption "July baby"; a picture posted by a child-actor-turned-author-turned-socialist-activist I'd met once ten years ago, of a book, with the caption "I wrote a book about imagining new politics, 'love' as an obfuscatory weapon, and why anxiety is good. Link in bio ($1.25)"; and a picture the founder of a once-hip media company had posted of a hand holding a glass of wine with the caption "some manicures deserve praise!"

I scrolled quickly to the top of my feed, swiping furiously downward with my thumb. I was swiping manically, and swiped a few extra times on accident, causing the top post to move down and a circling "refresh" icon to appear at the top of the screen.

Beneath the refresh icon, which disappeared when I stopped swiping, were the avatars and usernames of the people I followed, which I could tap to view their "stories."

•

Instagram stories were my favorite part of Instagram. Modeled loosely after Snapchat—an app on which I'd twice made an account, but which I'd never used—Instagram stories allowed users to post pictures and short videos to an auxiliary archive, available for twenty-four hours, which played in chronological order (pictures for ten seconds, videos for up to fifteen seconds) until manually stopped. I liked the impermanence of stories. Unlike Twitter, Facebook, and the main profile on Instagram, where the amalgamation of posts created a curated, there-unless-deleted archive, Instagram stories liberated one from the pressure of eternity. I often took pictures that were not good enough for my main page—they would look ugly next to my permanent pictures, were stylistically inconsistent with the general tone of my page, or were in some way embarrassing, offensive, or otherwise not suitable to be publicly archived—but that I nonetheless wanted to share. Instagram stories created a space for more marginal content, while decreasing the resultant anxiety of posting: only one-eighth of my followers regularly viewed my stories.

Sitting on the toilet, alternating between straining lightly and relaxing, I tapped the avatar of a writer I knew and began watching her story: a flyer for a workshop in Italy with red text that read "applications are still open—apply now"; a picture of a bone-thin woman posing suggestively near a table full of fancy-looking food; the same flyer for the workshop in Italy, this time from the workshop's Instagram account (I moved manually to the next post in the queue by tapping the right side of the screen); an advertisement for Sprint Mobile; a picture of a multiple-choice test on a screen with the circle filled in next to "Fear of death," with the text "Grad school v chill" superimposed at the bottom of the image; a selfie of someone next to a giant sunflower; another selfie of the same person next to flowers in a field; a video of water droplets moving on a flower petal; a video of a tape player playing what I thought was perhaps considered "shoegaze" music; feet walking on a shingled roof, the camera then panning upward to an expansive green field.

I began to tap feverishly through the posts without processing them, catching quick glimpses of faces, objects, and colors; I double-clicked the circle button at the bottom of my phone and swiped up, exiting everything. I shifted my weight onto my right, then left, cheek, before re-centering myself and straining. I opened Gmail and sent an email to Li—"pooping 'yet again'"—then double-clicked the circle button at the bottom of my phone and swiped up, closing Gmail.

My jaw unclenched, reminding me, impossibly, of a time in the far future when I would click my dentures together after having lost all my teeth in a war, the motion of my mouth coupling with the frantic intensity of Instagram to trigger vibratiuncles of false, future memory. I breathed out through my nose, letting my last resistance yield, as poop began to fall into the toilet.

Gratefully, I placed my phone on the rug at my feet; I strained a little, but for the most part felt that the work was being done for me. I closed my eyes and suddenly inhabited Violet's perspective, should she be awake and listening, noting with mild consternation my powerlessness over the sputtering sounds I was producing.

This was, so far, an average poop. The best poops were always on the cusp of diarrhea, the main difference—besides the feeling (diarrhea turbulently expelled, while the best poops soothingly emptied, though both with minimal waiting or strain)—was the wipe. Diarrhea was a pain to wipe, taking what felt like forever and using unseemly amounts of toilet paper, while the best poops often resulted in the much sought-after "one-and-done"—when the first wipe was also the last. Of course, I always double-checked after a one-and-done, so it was never truly only one and done, but the satisfaction lay less in the actual number of wipes and more in the knowledge one gleaned of oneself: that even in one's most archetypally unclean endeavor, one was clean.

If feelings exist to indicate the relative value of activities to us, a clean first wipe surely meant something good—after all, it felt good. And unlike other things that felt good only for a moment, followed by decline, or an urge to do the thing again, the glow after a one-and-done could last for an entire day. So I didn't hold it against myself that, for a time, I falsely believed that a one-and-done was causally correlated with a healthy diet. "The healthier I am, the cleaner my first wipe" was my mantra, but over time, my experience proved otherwise. I would often wipe clean after I'd eaten a whole pizza or an entire pint of ice cream, for example. This further decreased my faith in myself to make judgements: it was not always clear what caused things, even if—especially if—it seemed intuitively obvious, or felt good.

Like all learned things or new experiences, it took me some time to integrate this new information into my worldview. I wanted to believe that the times I ate greasy carbohydrates or an undignified amount of sugar and was graced with a one-and-done were aberrations; every time I ate cleanly then wiped clean only furthered my intuitive vision. Then I came to a crossroads that I simply could not ignore. I had been in New York for three days eating like an utter nihilist, eating pizza and french fries, pastries and meat and ice cream, and the whole time I was there I had pooped clean: not one single poop left a mess, even a little. This came as an unwelcome surprise; I hardly knew what to do with myself. Of course, the disconnect between my experiences and my worldview had been causing me low-level cognitive dissonance for quite some time—while I'd been able to dismiss most individual cases as exceptions, I'd never been able to fully discount them—and this made the matter much more plainly seen. If I hadn't been aware of the fact that there were ever exceptions, if I'd been willfully blind or merely inattentive, I likely would have missed it altogether.

My three-day streak in New York shattered my old presupposition so completely that for a while I'd become convinced that the opposite was true: the *unhealthier* I ate, the cleaner my first wipe would be. But it took me no time, relatively, to realize that this was just as absurd.

The truth was a third option which I hadn't previously had the willingness to grasp. Perhaps a clean first wipe had nothing to do with diet in any meaningful sense. There were many other factors than the single one with which I'd been analyzing my bowel movements—such as inflammation, the health of one's digestive tract, gallbladder and liver, the *color* of the food one ate, whether or not one has cancer, and more— and this had been a breakthrough; though it led to less certainty, I could at least begin to ask the right questions, and explore them from a more humble perspective.

Ultimately, however, a clean wipe was satisfying regardless of how it came to be or what it meant.

The bathtub faucet dripped thick drops into the basin, which splashed every second or so. The sound, when I was conscious of it, was maddening; it had begun to discomfit me—*pit-pat-pit-pat*— and I wanted to get up off the toilet. The problem could have easily been fixed by calling or texting the landlord, who would have gladly come or sent someone to fix it, but because I didn't want to deal with the resultant interaction, however brief or rel- atively painless, I'd been subjecting myself to this pitter-patter for months. It could also be solved by not pooping, I considered. The irksome, tinny plopping of the drips niggled me, and I was con- fronted by the fact of my negligent weakness in the face of potential social interaction—I wanted to leave the bathroom as quickly as possible.

"Fff," I sighed quietly, picking my phone up off the floor. I proceeded to open and close Ins- tagram and Twitter. Children started screaming outside in the street; I looked at my phone. There was nothing to click; I wanted something to click. I felt like I was trying to remember something.

I opened Twitter and tapped the search but- ton, then typed "Jordan Castro" in the search bar. I looked at Jordan Castro's Twitter frequently, but didn't follow him, because I didn't want to have to explain to anybody why I followed him. This was an Orwellian byproduct of the cross-contamination that occurred on Twitter: since users saw interactions between users they followed and users they didn't, based on a mysterious algorithm, this served not only as a way to introduce users to new content, but also as an auxiliary community watch—a kind of panopticon. It prevented me from clicking "like" on certain tweets; or following certain people—people like Jordan Castro.

Every conversation I'd had with people who didn't like Jordan Castro had been frustrating and unproductive; my inquisitors had more or less been incredulous and argumentative from the start, flagrantly mischaracterizing things they'd only thought he'd written or said, taking everything in bad faith, never having engaged properly with his work, and, most annoyingly of all, using rhetorical hyperbole instead of concrete language to express themselves. I did not want to waste any more of my time in hopeless non-conversation with closed-minded idiots who hated Jordan Castro—so I didn't follow him on Twitter.

I also didn't like getting distracted by his tweets. They were so interesting. It was wasteful enough getting sucked into Twitter by the vacuous, mind-deteriorating tweets of the people I followed, but it would be even more time consuming if I were to follow Jordan Castro: he tweeted multiple times per day and would often tweet links to long articles that required reading other articles to understand, or he would tweet something so compelling and strange I might spend a whole hour considering it, or he would post a picture of himself—he was beautiful—and so, though I'd find myself learning and thinking and admiring, I would also not be doing whatever it was I was supposed to be doing, like working on my novel.

I clicked on Jordan Castro's Twitter profile. His header photo was of three dirty bent-legged geese on pavement; it seemed almost like he'd uploaded it by accident. His profile picture was a line drawing that Russell Brill, the musician, had exhibited at an art gallery in his first and only show, titled *Canonical Paintings Drawn from Memory in Fifteen Minutes*—a rendition of Goya's *Saturn Devouring His Son*—which I'd learned about from an interview they'd done together.

Shifting my weight between buttocks on the toilet, I felt entirely uninterested in reading or thinking about anything; I felt preemptively exhausted at the prospect of being thrust into having to think about something; I needed to save my energy for my novel. I double-clicked the circle button at the bottom of my phone and swiped up, exiting Twitter. My face felt vaguely numb; my right leg tingled; I bounced my leg up and down on the ball of my foot, like a volatile invalid, or a child; it felt as if microscopic needles were pricking my calf and foot; I farted, which startled me.

The day had only just begun, I considered, communicating with myself without narrating my thoughts in language, experiencing them more organically, almost like colors: it wasn't too late to turn things around. When I finished pooping, I would go back to the kitchen and begin to work diligently on my novel. I bounced my right leg up and down; I was going to write a great novel; I was going to crush it; if I worked hard, minute by minute, day by day, I could write a novel I liked, perhaps even a novel I was proud of; I had the ability to change my life through my choices. This last insight came to me like a memory of something that had happened only moments ago; it surprised and delighted me—what an unbelievably great fact. I could finish pooping, wipe, wash my hands, walk into the kitchen, sit in front of my laptop, and work on my novel.

I opened the Notes application on my phone and opened a new note. "—" I wrote, then paused; "work on novel 2 hrs." I tapped the return key and typed "—" then paused again; "respond to emails," I wrote. The zeal with which I'd become convinced of my untrammeled capacity to act faded quickly; I imagined actually sitting down in front of my laptop; I was left with the familiar, timid creature of my will. I tapped the return key then half-heartedly typed "—"; but I couldn't think of what to type after.

I stared at my to-do list:

— work on novel 2 hrs.
— respond to emails
—

Before workdays, I made to-do lists at night, then woke up and completed tasks robotically. On my days off, when I had nothing to do except write, the construction of a to-do list could feel spiritlessly arbitrary, especially since it was so often executed in a last-ditch-effort style. So far my day was going horribly awry. I felt like I'd been listening to one loud continuous scream for minutes. Maybe I should just accept that the novel isn't going to happen, I considered. I could spend the day with Violet; we could go somewhere she wanted to go . . .

Violet liked going to places like museums, historical sites, parks, cemeteries, mansions, and other places, whereas I tended not to like going anywhere. I could muster up some resolve, accept the fact that I had started off my day stuntedly, was not on track to recover; I could utilize my free time to nourish my relationship. My shoulders and neck tensed; I un-tensed them.

Relax, I thought slowly—reellaaaaaaaxxxx.

I recalled with humble reticence mine and Violet's most recent attempt at going somewhere together, when she'd taken me to a mansion that contained, among other things, the world's largest collection of Fabergé eggs. I hadn't wanted to go, had no interest in mansions or Fabergé eggs or in going for any other reason—I'd been planning to work on my novel all day—but it had been a while since we'd done something fun and I knew we were due for an outing, so I agreed to go.

Immediately, I'd been struck by how many old people were swarming the mansion, which, though notably large, was rather gaudy and inelegant. It seemed as if a bus had just come from a nursing home and dropped off all its patients; the old people seemed lost; milling about, waiting, I'd gleaned, for a tour guide. Violet and I had inquired about a tour, then decided not to wait, walking endlessly through the long halls, entering and exiting rooms that contained vast amounts of clumsily organized and giant-seeming furniture and gold and silver objects. I'd had a hard time believing that anybody could truly care about such rooms and objects; walking through the maze-like halls with Violet, stopping occasionally to stare at ostensibly beautiful things, I felt only a desire to leave as quickly as possible. Every time Violet looked at me I would smile what I was certain she could tell was a forced smile, her head turning to look at me, and my mouth suddenly, as though shocked, curling too quickly, eyes widening, cheeks rigid.

What did I like to do? I considered abstractedly, on the toilet, pained by my memory of our failed adventure. Was doing things really so important? I felt my mind defensively fragment and scatter; I was immediately overwhelmed, then numb; I sensed that there was nothing I could simply *think* while sitting here that had the power to defeat this self-assault, which I already felt coming on. Trying to deflect by thinking about my novel, but accidentally proceeding with my initial concern, I remembered reading a book titled *The Art of Being*, about the "poetics of the novel and existentialist philosophy," in which the author wrote about Kierkegaard's review of some Hans Christian Andersen novels, wherein Kierkegaard accused Andersen of not being a "real novelist." What was important, for Kierkegaard, was that a novel have a "life-view"; a question like "Is life really meaningful?" could spread out infinitely, consuming its subject, unanswered; whereas a question like "How can I live a meaningful life?" implied an active commitment to reality, which everything conformed around. The truth of life was not an idea, but something more akin to a living personality, dynamically engaged in the process of life. Asking the wrong questions would result in disjointed, world-weary meandering, or inaction. The wrong questions made novels that bled out into life, and lives that bled into novels: everything a lukewarm soup of fragmented, poetic moods. The wrong questions consumed, rather than gave. Over years, I'd begun to suspect that I was motivated to stay stuck inside these kinds of questions out of fear. Without an active disposition toward life, or a unifying life-task, I was absolved of my responsibility to step forward, into my own life, and could languish in front of my laptop, *thinking*, eschewing all else for the sake of my "novel," pretending that I was engaged in something important and unique, when in reality I was engaged in common cowardice.

I tried to draw these thoughts into my mind, thinking, Novelist . . . when I noticed my feet slightly tingling, almost asleep, so I wiggled them.

To my delight, I had finished pooping. I didn't know how, but I knew I was done. I'd actually forgotten that I had been sitting on the toilet in the first place. I put my phone next to my feet, twisted my torso, grabbed the toilet paper roll from on top of the toilet tank, unraveled four or five squares, ripped at the perforated edge, twisted my torso to place the roll back on the tank, then folded what I had in my hands.

Specs of dust floated through the lighted air in front of me as I fondled the folded, rather dry, toilet paper. The roll was from a 7-Eleven four-pack, not my favorite, in fact a brand I loathed, but which I used when necessary, if I ran out at night and other stores weren't open, or when I didn't have enough money to buy it in bulk. It was a self-perpetuating cycle: when I purchased such a small quantity, I ran out more frequently, and I always seemed to run out at night.

This inferior toilet paper was textured in such a way that when enough pressure was applied, small fibers got caught in my hairs, and frazzled. It never ripped through to the hand (an event which had traumatized me in childhood—I'd become convinced for days after the incident, which had happened at school, that my hand smelled and someone would notice; I'd faked sick, skipped class, had a panic attack, stayed home for days, and when I went back to school I put my hands in my pockets and looked down, an act that would go on to characterize much of my young adulthood, all because of inadequate toilet paper—and which caused me, perhaps most importantly of all, to wipe with caution throughout the rest of my life), but nonetheless it caught and frayed, leaving small bits of white, like fuzz, in my butt crack.

So, I made sure to apply pressure carefully while wiping, once, from front to back; my legs buzzed as I leaned forward, my thighs pressing into the rounded edge of the seat; the nerve endings in my hamstrings sent vibrations through my legs, up through my arms, then briefly to my face; my entire body microscopically quivered for one or two seconds. I checked.

The toilet paper was clean!

Still, I wanted to double-check. Preparing to tear off a few more squares, I noted unhappily, and not for the first time, that the roll was unusually small. Was the thickness of the individual squares an attempt to keep one buying more? A small roll, made even smaller due to the thickness of the ostensibly two-ply toilet paper, would surely increase sales; perhaps the cyclical trap I fell into when I purchased this toilet paper had been 7-Eleven's sinister plan all along . . .

I tore some more squares at the perforated edge and began folding. Everything in convenience stores was like that; the value of the products wasn't the quality, or quantity, but the convenience; small bottles of Listerine for $3.49; three-packs of condoms for $4.00; a four-pack of small toilet paper rolls for $5.95; all readily available, day or night . . . I stood and turned around, facing the toilet, in anticipation of another clean wipe, then bent my knees and hips slightly, and wiped once more with aplomb.

My morale, however, was short-lived. I brought the toilet paper around and beheld, to my dismay, a soiled square. I folded it hastily and, still standing, wiped. How could this be? I checked again: the right side of the toilet paper was streaked! I made to sit down, bending my knees, but stopped and remained standing: I would finish this now, I resolved.

Sometimes the right side of my butt required more wipes than the left or the middle; it was a pattern I'd passively noticed for years; I pondered the possible explanations for this strange fact as I stood above the toilet, bent slightly at the hips.

Poop, I imagined, came out more or less uniformly, barely touching the cheeks. And even when it didn't squeeze and slide, but rather plopped and plunked, the splattering impact on the water would only, in extreme cases, touch the rounded outer cheeks, not the inner crack-adjacent cheeks where the wiping took place. Mine this morning had been evenly paced; no rubbing or smushing or plopping or splash-causing spattering happened at all.

Yet, my problem remained.

I tossed the soiled toilet paper into the bowl, ripped another few folded sheets, and wiped again. I moved my right hand, my wiping hand, in front of me to see the damage: an ever-so-slight streak of brown on the right—pastel, like a watercolor.

This was progress; I was fairly certain I could get away with not wiping again, but I'd come this far, and desired, as anyone would, the satisfaction of seeing, on the paper, *full clean*. It was the same satisfaction, I imagined, of standing over the freshly dead body of one's enemy. I folded the toilet paper over onto itself; this would hopefully be the final time; my fingers moved; then something wonderfully illuminating came to me. The reason the right side was often more streaked than the left was not because of the way the poop came out—it had nothing to do with that at all—but because of the way I'd been wiping! I could feel as I wiped now that I applied pressure unevenly, because I wiped with my right hand and brought the toilet paper around my right side to check; my fingers were different lengths and strengths; my middle finger, the finger that swiped my right cheek during each wipe, was the longest and strongest of all; the extra pressure likely pressed the poop deeper into my hair, rubbing it in firmly, causing it to stick to or smear against my skin, creating an ever-increasing need for more wipes, as opposed to the proper amount of pressure from my less dominant fingers, which merely wiped it off as intended. It was something I'd been unaware that I was doing all along.

My final wipe was indeed clean; I tossed it into the bowl and pressed the cold silver lever.

The tea was the perfect temperature as I sipped and sat down, greeting the mild warmth with my mouth and throat, brightening the screen and maximizing the internet, which presented itself to me the way I'd left it: with my novel pulled up and no other tabs open. I read the first few sentences too quickly, then read them again. My brain was buzzing; I felt like I was wearing a backpack, the sentences squeezing my shoulders and pulling me down. I read some sentences again, hating them, despairing over their tense and point of view, realizing with horror that all of the words looked inexcusably hideous, clunking up against each other clumsily, making no real sense—the first few sentences of my novel were an unbearable atrocity. I quickly opened a new tab, went to Twitter, exited Twitter, went to Gmail, exited Gmail, then opened a new Google Doc. I moved the cursor into the box that said "Untitled" and typed "novel first person"; deleted that and typed "novel"; deleted that and typed "nov"; then deleted that and typed "novel 1st person."

I copied and pasted my novel into the new document. I began manually changing the perspective—each "he" to "I," "him" to "me," "his" to "mine"—but after the first four sentences I paused, took two sips then one large gulp of tea, and realized, due to the familiar chalkiness and strangely textured mouthfeel of the gulp, that I had reached the end. I glanced into the mug to confirm, then stood and made my way toward the counter.

The french press, in theory, contained 32 ounces of liquid, 2.65 mugs' worth, but in reality it contained closer to 2.3. The discrepancy was due to how many tea leaves I used, the mass of which created its own approximately 4.4-ounce layer at the bottom of the french press; so, anticipating the amount that would be left over, I filled my mug from the french press at the counter and drank three large sips while standing there, then "topped off" my mug with what was left, approximately .3 ounces, thinking, "top it off, top it off, top it off," imagining myself in a rap music video, surrounded by floating money and shaking butts, drinking tea. I greedily sipped the tea, still the perfect temperature, as I made my way toward the table, spine preemptively hunched in anticipation of putting the mug down and sitting, which I did, then rubbed my eyes, sat up straight, exhaled loudly, and continued manually changing the tense of my novel.

After what felt like ten minutes, but was actually only three, I read what I had changed so far and stopped. It didn't sound nearly as good in first person. Perhaps the sentences, which had actually sounded so good, I realized now, in third person, were dependent on the breathy *h* and the stern-sounding *im* and *ee* of "him" and "he," and did not translate well to the first person, "I." Distractedly, I recalled an article I'd half-read—or was it a quote I'd seen on Twitter?—about how first person present tense had been historically viewed as less literary; I struggled to think of any books written in the first person present tense that weren't written by Bret Easton Ellis. *Chilly Scenes of Winter* by Ann Beattie was in the third person present tense, I considered, unhelpfully. First person present tense . . . Céline? I'd only read around one hundred pages of *Death on the Installment Plan*, which I couldn't remember anything about, except that maybe it had been written in the first person present tense. I rested my hands on the base of my laptop and recalled with a shudder the time I'd told Li and another friend, an academic and memoirist—who'd once confided in me that he thought Céline was "the greatest novelist of all time"—that I'd copied the entirety of *Less Than Zero* by Bret Easton Ellis word for word in a document in an attempt to learn the style. We were at dinner and I had wanted to impress them; this did not impress them. It was also a lie. I hadn't actually copied the whole thing, just some pages, though I'd intended to copy the whole thing. The academic and memoirist had said, "Really?" then said he didn't like Bret Easton Ellis. I said something about "just liking the style," trying my best to conceal my then admiration for Bret Easton Ellis. I remembered too that my boss had once made fun of Hunter S. Thompson for copying *The Great Gatsby* word for word, and felt embarrassed for having thought that this was something worth doing, let alone lying about. Sitting at my kitchen table, I refocused my eyes on my novel. It sucked.

I tried to think of a book to model my novel after, but couldn't. When people learned to play the guitar, they learned other people's songs first, before they wrote their own. What made this any different?

Feeling self-conscious and adrenaline filled, like a novice bank robber backing away from the teller, I began changing my novel from present to past tense. There were plenty of novels in first person past tense, I considered, which would make it easier to find one to study, and would allow for more stylistic choices; I changed "is" to "was," feeling hopeful.

I wanted my first novel to be taken seriously. I thought of my friend who'd said that he didn't trust third person writing and felt confident now: he would trust my now first person past tense book. Many people will like my book now that it is in first person past tense, I rejoiced. I took a sip of tea.

Finally, my novel was coming along.

After reworking the entire first paragraph, nearly a page, I read what I'd changed of my novel so far;

it was undoubtedly worse than before. It wasn't clear why, or from where, the story was being told; everything felt less active.

But it wasn't less active, I considered. First person was the perspective of choice, of deliberative interpretation, of action; in first person, there were stakes; first person was, in the end, the perspective of life. Life was lived in the present tense, interpreted in the past tense, with an eye to the future tense—but always in first person. This was one major difference between literature and life, I considered: while reading a novel, one could inhabit another first person consciousness without the usual burden of first-personal deliberation. In this way, the defining feature of first person perspective was removed, so one could suspend their own first person consciousness, with all its active doubts and decisions, and take on another momentarily. However, I considered, sitting at my kitchen table, touching my face, if deliberative interpretation was what characterized the first person perspective of life, and it was removed from the first person perspective of literature, there was really nothing fundamentally first personal about it. First person was, in literature, I thought, the same as third person, both were fundamentally third personal, and so both of my novel documents were actually exactly the same.

Stressed, I closed the tab containing my new first person past tense novel, then opened a new tab and clicked Twitter; I closed Twitter and scrolled down to an arbitrary place in my original novel and began reading. Fuck.

"Fuck . . ." I whispered, nodding my head up and down, then rolling it back, staring up at the ceiling. I pushed my tongue between my teeth and clamped down.

I looked at my novel. The end of the second paragraph on the page that I'd scrolled to had a nice cliff-hanger-style ending—when Calvin is sitting in his study with a hippie kid he worked with named Fingers, who'd just begun talking about "blowing someone's face off"—but there were four more paragraphs below it, so I pressed the return key until the four paragraphs were on their own page: a new chapter. Short chapters were the only aspect of my novel I felt confident about. Everything about most novels seemed oppressive; I didn't want my novel to oppress anyone; short chapters weren't oppressive.

I scrolled down to the new chapter and read the first two sentences. The two sentences explained that to "blow someone's face off" meant to blow a large quantity of pure LSD from the palm of your hand into another person's face, causing them to lose their personality. The sentences sounded fine, but the fact that the novel was in third person present tense made everything feel lifeless and thin. What was I going to do? There seemed to be something buzzing behind my face; thick liquid oozing through my skull, through my shoulders and neck, encasing my brain; no matter how badly I wanted to calmly and methodically work on my novel, whatever thoughts I needed, wherever they came from, got stuck in this goo casing and couldn't get through to my brain; the only things already inside the casing were distressingly cyclical thoughts about the point of view and tense of my novel.

Discouraged by my spastic, unproductive behavior, I decided to reorient myself by sending some emails: perhaps completing a small task would ground me and encourage more confident, decisive action. I opened Gmail. Li had emailed me again. "Fuck off," the email said, simply.

I grinned and responded, "Floundering this morning. Feel like I'm flopping . . . Trying to work on novel."

I closed the internet then opened it, momentarily unable to recall what I had been trying to do, impulsively misfiring due to the burst of energy I felt from my email correspondence. I stood up and walked into the living room. The mirror on the mantle, which reflected the room, was flattering; it leaned against the wall in such a way, pointed slightly upward, as to make me look thinner and stronger; my face looked less round, my chest and shoulders broader. I flexed my chest and shoulders and turned sideways, flexed my triceps, then turned to face the mirror. Body . . . I thought, hesitantly. Body man, I confirmed. Sup brotha, I thought, inhabiting a memory of an Italian kid I vaguely knew from Cleveland, who always said, "Sup, brotha." I touched my hair and made a face. "Yo," I mouthed, moving my body, imagining myself as a rapper onstage. I walked into the kitchen, to the counter; half-filled a cup with water from the sink and drank it; I imagined I could feel the water flowing through each part of my body, one at a time; it was stimulating, then calming; shocking, then soothing; I filled another few sips' worth and drank it. The morning was receding into some point in the distance; diminishing into nothing; replaced by an incessant, microscopic gnawing, tense shoulders, and an increased heart rate.

Fuck. Fuck fuck.

Maybe I should go for a run? Or to the coffee shop? I could walk in the woods, I considered. I wanted to work on my novel, but felt increasingly doomed. I should definitely leave the house. I didn't have enough money in my bank account to justify spending on coffee; a run was probably just what I needed, but it felt, in some sense, like giving up.

I'd always assumed that people were in control of their behavior, that their thoughts and actions lined up, or were causally related, but this just isn't true: we experience mysterious phenomena, then narrate that phenomena to ourselves as best we can, using language and other images; then we try to read our own minds, just as we try to read other people's—we do not *think* then act; the relationship between thinking and acting is not at all a straight line. The totality of oneself—only a small portion of which is conscious thought— acts, and in order to have even a slim chance of interpretation one must observe oneself.

For example, part of me knew that if I consumed more caffeine while feeling anxious and directionless, the caffeine would only serve to amplify those feelings, but another entertained the possibility that more caffeine could help me work on my novel. I walked toward the counter, where I paused and exhaled tragically, then reached up and removed the measuring cup from the shelf; filled it with two cups of water, then poured the water into the electric kettle.

We must "choose" ourselves too, I considered. Self-knowledge was not enough. It was still possible, after all, to choose in contradiction to what one sees, or "knows," or thinks he wants. I conceived of my desire as a string, being pulled by whatever I was ultimately oriented toward. My thoughts were embedded in something much larger and harder to fathom than my tiny, cramped kitchen. I looked down at my hands.

When my consciousness sharpened, I retroactively heard water splashing against water: had the kettle been full when I poured the water into it? I lifted the kettle to gauge its weight; it was heavier than if it had only contained two cups. I dumped it into the sink and repeated the process. Then I turned the kettle on.

Hearing the ssshhhhh of the kettle starting to boil the water behind me, I walked back to the table, sat, and half-consciously navigated from Twitter to YouTube. I sensed that I was taking concrete action toward an unconscious end, then resolved—and even began to feel physically relaxed, adding post hoc intention ongoingly—to watch something while I waited for the water to boil. The decision to watch something always brought me some relief. I typed "Jordan Castro social media" into the YouTube search bar, hoping to find a clip of him reading something about social media, either to justify my erratic use or to inspire me to think differently about it, but since most of the videos were readings and interviews ranging from forty minutes to three hours long, or had to do with other people named Jordan Castro, I clicked one titled "Jordan Castro Internet -- REMIXX (fan video)" on the sixth results page, the thumbnail of which showed Jordan Castro's head superimposed on a black background with purple and green neon laser beams crisscrossing behind it.

The video began instrumentally; a cartoon serpent slithered in place; Jordan Castro's attractive head floated toward it on a magic carpet, then his voice came overlaid on top of the music, cut from what I assumed was an interview. "Because of the way people process and interact with their political opinions now, their political opinions have become ruinously linked with their personalities to an unprecedented degree. Whereas before, it was uncouth to ask others who they voted for, or what they believed, now people process and interact with their political opinions immediately, in public, all the time, on a platform designed to addict them, so instead of thinking in any meaningful sense about what they think, feel, and believe, people are more or less always self-consciously performing, and becoming addicted to that performance." Jordan Castro's disembodied head bounced around on the screen; the electronic trance music was, I intuited, going to build until the beat dropped—it sounded bad.

I felt distantly embarrassed, imagining Violet catching me watching the video. "Now, people conflate their opinions with their personalities, and not only that, they conflate their opinions with that part of their personalities that specifically seeks to be liked." The word "liked" reverberated; the music stopped—then the beat dropped.

"People want to be liked more than anything." I couldn't tell if the voice was Jordan Castro's voice or someone else reading something
he'd written. "People have always wanted to be
liked. But today, people want to be liked more
than anything." This music was thumping now.
"People want to be liked; not just by their family, or their friends, or their classmates, or their
coworkers, but by everybody. Since everything is
processed in public, on social media—the same
place where people post selfies with pursed lips,
and curate their personas to reflect, on the whole,
what they think is the most desirable version of
themselves (a version meant for immediate consumption and likes)—people's opinions have
begun to reflect exactly this, mirroring more
closely the opinions they want others to think
they have, rather than the opinions that they actually have."

I turned down the volume, already low
but accosting me nonetheless; Jordan's head
emerged from a volcano and lava shot out of his
eyes and mouth; a cartoon bodybuilder body
emerged on the left side of the screen, then slid
across the screen until it met with Jordan's head,
attaching itself to his head and then dancing. I

considered how he overemphasized "opinions," which seemed, to me, wholly unimportant.

"People don't know the difference between the opinions others want them to have and the opinions that they actually have; people mistake how they think they should think for how they actually think, and how they want to seem for how they are. *People mistake how they think they should think for how they actually think, and how they want to seem for how they are. People mistake how they think they should think for how they actually think, and how they want to seem for how they are.*" This line repeated many times, the song mimicking a DJ scratching turntables each time it repeated. I felt a self-conscious confusion—it was morning, this was how I was spending my morning—then, inexplicably, I felt inspired to work on my novel.

The sound of Jordan's voice and the music seemed to soften, as if it were taking up less space, or had moved to a different compartment in my consciousness, as my eyes blurred and I turned inward, vaguely considering my novel. I sat for fifteen or so seconds, mouth open, the song sharpening and softening, cutting in and out of my direct mental experience. "Everybody, essentially, just wants to be liked," I heard from the laptop, which sounded like it was coming from somewhere behind or inside of the wall. Jordan Castro's mouth opened and there was an effect of falling endlessly through it; in the background, dancing trolls wiggled atop bent-up cars; images from memes I only dimly recognized appeared; the video started flashing like a strobe light and, sitting at my kitchen table, I watched mostly unfeelingly as the video stopped abruptly and an advertisement started playing automatically, the water boiling behind and to the right of me.

I turned in my seat toward the boiling water to check the temperature as the advertisement played—a vague, glowing redness on the base of the kettle. I felt kind of creeped out by the video. What kind of person would make something like this? Jordan Castro fans seemed troubled. I considered the sentiments expressed in the video. It did seem true that everybody, more or less, wanted to be liked, but it didn't seem like a worthwhile endeavor to make a damaged neon laser video about it. I doubted if people wanted to be liked now more than before, but I guessed it was possible. Did people in ancient civilizations, or pre-civilization, seek mainly to be liked? They sought to be liked by God, it occurred to me, weakly. There was utility in being liked . . . I often engaged with my novel anxiously, from the point of view of *another*—when I edited my novel, was what I mainly felt a fear of not being liked? No. Of course, people had always liked me . . . But was it because I'd wanted them to, and tried to get them to?

Nonexistent other . . . I thought, thinking at first that I was remembering the name of a metal band, then realized I wasn't.

People mistake how they think they should think for how . . . I couldn't remember the sentence exactly. Even though the video was aesthetically unsettling in the most profound sense, "fried" in every sense of the word, it didn't seem exactly bad that it existed. There was so much I'd categorically dismissed because I found it aesthetically displeasing; I often wondered if my entire worldview when I was young had been based on aesthetics rather than the kinds of ideological convictions I'd imagined myself having. Maybe my worldview had just been based on the wrong aesthetics? How did one choose what one engaged with or ignored? Did one even choose? My eyes blurred and my head tilted back; I suddenly imagined a future in which I tweeted my opinions and reactions uninhibitedly, this future vision springing forth from nothing, like someone popping out of the bushes.

"Weak . . . pop culture–obsessed . . . self-indulgent . . . children . . ." I mumbled grumpily, like an old man, rolling my head back down, staring down now, struggling to articulate something about those who increasingly comprised the corner of the so-called literary world I inhabited, and who I'd imagined reacting negatively to my fantasy tweets, sitting at my kitchen table. I daydreamed about unleashing the *true whig* on Twitter; tweeting belligerently, embracing the most fried aspects of myself; alienating myself permanently from the so-called literary world, who famously did not like jokes, did not understand jokes; who did not like having to think, and who ultimately hated smiling. Before, I'd felt convinced that there were readers out there who would embrace me; now I felt convinced that there were not. Mouth open, eyes blurred, neck bent, head lolled to the side, I considered that even if I did finish my novel, there would be nobody to read it.

I thought of the people who I met when I first started writing. There were no individual thinkers among them, save Li and a few others. My old peers, who I'd thought were so interesting and interested in thinking, who I'd misunderstood as being fundamentally weird, were, in reality, not interesting or interested in thinking or weird at all—they were entirely stupid and normal. Most writers, or writer types—most of them were not even really writers, but rather, *writer types*—are not weird at all; in fact, they are utterly normal, I thought, sitting at my kitchen table. They order a quirky drink at Starbucks, or wear slightly oversized glasses, or something else cosmetic, and all of their jokes, the entirety of their humor, and all of their output, their corrupt and childish output, which is anything but literary, is predicated on this ornamental weirdness, this faux individuality—they produce nothing substantial, nothing that doesn't point back to themselves and their precious quirks. The punch line of every joke they tell is always *Haha! Look at me! I'm so weird!* but this weirdness functions only to point back to what is normal; the point of everything they write is *Hey! Hey! Look at me! I'm so weird! What do you think of me?*

I was narrating my thoughts to myself in full sentences now, almost like I was writing, perhaps as a result of watching the video, the tone of which had seeped into my consciousness. I recalled one person in particular who I'd met through writing years ago, who I'd initially thought was a writer but who had over time proven herself to be merely a *writer type*; she had written one inconsequential book of aphorisms, then became—like so many wealthy, arts-adjacent aphorists—an "activist."

Undifferentiated and only cosmetically varied, the literary world had become one swarming mass, like a rat king. Their cosmetic differences hid a frightened, stifled sameness, which sought only more of itself, and which cast out any true difference, often in the name of difference, while pretending, even to itself, that it didn't know what it was doing. Any time a group wasn't sufficiently differentiated, I knew, it aggressively descended into delusion; in which case only those who firmly stood outside could see the truth. The crowd is untruth . . . I thought, remembering the title of a Kierkegaard essay.

A hazy acknowledgment that I wasn't being very wise emanated from a place that felt at once inside and beside me, as I moved my finger toward the trackpad and touched it. I clicked Twitter and the first tweet on my feed, unsurprisingly, was hers, this *writer type*. I'd been wanting to unfollow her for years, but hadn't, because of, it occurred to me now, the desire to be liked, and to maintain my perceived social status in a specific social group. I was, as would occasionally reveal itself to me in moments like these, pathetic. The tweet read "white women need to calm down" above a picture of two celebrities I didn't recognize. I clicked her profile.

Thumb-sucker, I thought, delighted, surprising myself and smiling. Look at this . . . thumb-sucker, I thought. Beneath the picture of the celebrities was a tweet from an editor at a prestigious publishing house who I didn't follow, which showed up in my feed due to the Californian writer type having liked it.

I clicked the editor's profile. These weak, sniveling pastry eaters . . . These . . . I felt feral and aggressive, while simultaneously numb and resigned. The editor's most recent tweet said "Eating some shrimp chimps, about to go BANANAS on a manuscript." Gross, I thought. Ew. Did she mean shrimp chips? *Shrimp chimps?* I imagined the editor smacking her lips together, like a cow chewing cud, moving her head back and forth, smiling stupidly, struggling to open a bag of shrimp chips; reaching her hand into the bag, pulling out a shrimp chip, and stuffing it into her mouth. I felt disgusted. Did she really eat chips while editing? The shrimp chip grease on her fingers, her fingers on her keyboard, smearing the shrimp chip grease on her keyboard then touching her face, eating another shrimp chip, picking up a piece of paper, crossing something out . . .

The literary world was full of poisoned people, who, for all of their concern about this or that *issue*, seemed totally unconcerned about the issue of their own unseemliness, I thought. This would have been fine, I considered, in the past, when you didn't have to think about it; when editors were just editors, and weren't shrimp chip gobblers, constantly brutalizing everyone with their barefaced shrimp chimp *pride*; when you could simply know people in their professional capacities, and did not have to imagine all the grease that permanently dripped from their delighted, shiny lips and hands. Yes, those were the days, I thought; unlike now, when one was forced to ponder how people's keyboards even worked—all of those greasy, wiggling digits, creeping greedily toward stickered laptops, slipping and sliding on the screens of their phones . . .

After consuming the horrific tweet, I reflexively clicked out of Twitter, out of the whole internet, and, back at my laptop desktop, opened the internet again and clicked Gmail. I simply wasn't supposed to see things like that, I thought. It was totally undignified. I felt frustrated bodily, as if the tweet about shrimp chimps had manifested itself as a tangible tension in my upper back. More likely, I considered, later, while writing about it, the sensation was the result of constant empty clicks over a long period of time acting on my brain; the long-term psychological effects of clicking to see if there is anything new, any new likes, any new content, or clicking unconsciously for "no reason," not even cognizant of the clicking, countless times throughout the day, every day, in a zombie-like or fiendish manner; most of the time seeing nothing new, having no new likes; the physical manifestation of so many days like this, one after another, for years—this tension.

I focused my eyes and realized that I had my phone in my hand and was looking at Twitter, having, apparently, unconsciously navigated to it, looking at the "white women need to calm down" tweet again; over a period of milli-seconds, I began feeling increasingly like I was seeing from my "second face," blurrily interpret-ing the contents on the screen, as I clicked the tweet, which had 164 retweets and 385 likes, and scrolled briefly through the list of users who'd liked it, none of whom I recognized.

I had heard the kettle whir, around 135 degrees, when I'd begun to watch the Jordan Castro video, then stopped hearing it until I noticed its absence. During the interim, around 140–204 degrees, the hum of the kettle had blended into the sounds of the kitchen—the groan of the water heater, the rumble of the furnace, the occasional creak of the fridge—then drowned "into" itself; I adjusted my position in the chair and turned my head and upper body toward the kettle, straining my ears to make sure—it had stopped. I scooted my chair back and got up from the table, jerking my stiff body toward the kettle, then jolting to a halt; I bent my hips and moved my hand toward my lap-top, intending, bizarrely, to close it, but instead only clicking out of the internet, then standing upright and more or less scurrying toward the counter.

The water was 185 degrees; not 205, just before the boiling point, where it needed to be for brewing coffee; it must have stopped earlier and had time to cool down. I turned it on again. This time the *ssshhhh* began instantly, rising like the inverse of a wave after crashing, making a sound not dissimilar to the *ssshhooooppp* that occurred during sped-up movie rewinds—a man steps forward out of his office into the end-of-day sunlight, then *shhhoooopppppp*, it quickly rewinds to the beginning of the day and starts again in real time, but this time, on his way to work, he drops his phone and, as a result, everything changes. I watched the red numbers spike—185, 188, 191—then plateau around 195, taking longer and longer between single degrees, which reminded me of something my father said once. "It's harder to make one million dollars than it is to make ten million," he'd told me, at an age when I didn't understand or want to understand anything about money, or listen to anything my father told me. I thought about that in terms of the glowing red numbers on the base of the kettle, struggling in smaller increments after increasing quickly at first—I wondered if it wasn't some kind of rule or law, that things excel at first, then plateau and have more trouble advancing near the top, before realizing, disoriented, that his comment suggested the opposite. I sighed and looked down at the red numbers: 194. I remembered a stand-up comedian's joke:

"Who was it that said the first million was the hardest?"

[pause]

"Was it Hitler?"

The red numbers on the digital screen blinked from 198 back to 195, up to 199 then down to 198 again quickly. I retrieved the Chemex-brand bonded filters from the cupboard, then pulled one from the box and placed it as best I could onto the mouth of the Chemex—unfolding one layer from the folded paper square to make a sort of cone, then placing it into the mouth of the Chemex—however, due to the lack of a binding agent, the lazily coned filter resumed its original square shape almost immediately and sort of slid, then teetered uneasily, against the side of the mouth of the Chemex.

The Chemex, an hourglass-shaped flask with a conical neck and a wooden collar, was useful for making more than one cup of coffee at a time—whereas the more popular pour-over contraptions, like the Hario V6o, produced only one. The problem was that if you made more than one cup in the Chemex (unless you were making it for more than one person), you would be forced to stand for several minutes, arm aching, mind racing, preparing the coffee, only to end up with a cold second cup (provided you didn't suck it down so quickly as to not taste the coffee at all). There was probably some kind of sleeve, like a beer koozie, I considered, standing over my utensils at the counter, that one could get to keep the coffee in the Chemex warm, but I knew that I wouldn't look into it: I never bought gadgets or superfluous kitchen items; it never occurred to me to do so except at the exact moment I needed them, after which the thought would immediately leave my mind.

The Chemex was also inconvenient to clean. The shape was not conducive to the classic sponge; it was impossible to fit a whole hand through the neck (unless you had a tiny deformed hand, or you were a small child); it was not conducive to the kind of sponge that was attached to a handle, because, though it fit through the neck, it was difficult to properly torque—the handle bumping clunkily up against the glass, the sponge barely reaching the base—which made it nearly impossible to press with sufficient force; so after an invariably arduous effort, a dark, private struggle, nothing, ultimately, would get truly clean. Thus, I'd resigned myself to using a defeated, lackadaisical method: I squirted a small amount of soap into the Chemex, then held it under hot water, swirling and occasionally emptying the soapy water into the sink. This seemed to work fine, except that there remained the residual smell of old coffee in the flask, which, I intuited, created a less-fresh cup of coffee, and perhaps even exponentially less-fresh cups of coffee over time. Often, I would forego cleaning the Chemex altogether—diminishing returns—and merely rinse the flask once after I used it, then once more before the next time.

Holding the Chemex now beneath the faucet, I rinsed the inside quickly then dumped the water out into the sink. The light-brown streaks on the bottom of the glass glinted as I shook the flask to get the last water droplets out. I moved the Chemex toward my face and my face toward the Chemex, until my nose hovered over the opening; I inhaled deeply; it smelled like stale coffee;

I turned the sink on and rinsed the Chemex out once more.

I placed the filter back onto the mouth of the flask, but this time I fingered it more firmly, shaping the paper into its desired conicality and loosely holding it in place. I looked at the kettle—203 degrees—then removed it from the base and poured a small quantity of water onto the filter in a circular motion. This acted as a binding agent, holding the filter in place, but it also removed any sediment from the filter, which, if not rinsed, would taint the taste of the eventual cup, or cups, of coffee.

It ultimately didn't matter though, since my Chemex wasn't clean.

I plucked the filter from the Chemex, holding it between my thumb and pointer finger, and poured the water that had dripped through into the sink, then secured the filter into its position on the flask again.

I weakly half-hummed a made-up tune, which emerged from my mouth as a series of exasperated sighs, as I retrieved a bag of coffee beans from the shelf jutting out of the side of the cupboard, then shook the bag to gauge the amount of beans left, though I'd purchased them the day before. I gently peeled back the thin flaps of cardboard that kept the bag closed; I uncurled the top of the bag.

The scent entered my nostrils; I imagined my face in sunshine, elated, mouth wide; I imagined everything shaking in sunlight, like an earthquake; I put my nose over the bag to get a better whiff; the beans smelled succulent. I shook the bag and smelled the beans again, mechanically, shaking and sniffing, microscopically quivering as I inhaled the chocolatey-caramel aroma. I lamented my lack of a scale as I poured some beans into a measuring cup, filling it up to half a cup—roughly the equivalent, according to a Reddit thread I'd read about brewing coffee, of twenty-four grams of coffee.

I poured the beans into the grinder and pressed grind, which instantly produced a loud, frankly alarming, noise, and I thought of Violet; it sounded like a terrorist attack; I imagined ducking for cover, bullets flying all around me; I hoped the noise wouldn't wake her. I was aware of my teeth touching. I stared at the wall behind and to the right of the grinder, my brain blankly diminishing into a small point inside of itself, or into the wall in front of me, as if trying to block out both the noise and the potential of the noise waking Violet, as well as the potential guilt of waking her up—I suddenly imagined fingers emerging from the wall and wiggling toward me, and I began to move my hand toward the grind button to stop it—then the noise stopped on its own.

A friend, a few years prior, had given me his book collection, and in it, among the many books I knew I would never read, was The Joy of Coffee. It was a wide book and didn't fit neatly onto any of my shelves, so I left it on my coffee table and occasionally flipped through it, one day entertaining the thought that acquiring a new hobby might make me less depressed: I decided to read the book. After reading the first page, however, I quickly became bored; I was unable to translate the words I'd read into their associated meanings; I hated everything; I wondered how and why people were so interested in coffee, in anything really, and how and why people wrote books like this. At the time, I'd felt incapable of sustained interest in anything outside of myself and my immediate desires, which were constricted and circular; it felt as if my thoughts needed to inhabit some fuller act of the imagination that they were incapable of accessing on their own; and so I grasped at things haphazardly, such as this coffee book, which didn't work. One thing I did remember though, from flipping through the book over the years, was the importance of letting coffee "bloom" when one prepared it. "Blooming" consisted of pouring a small amount of water over the ground beans and waiting approximately thirty seconds as they rose, thereby releasing the more intricate flavors. It was really rather beautiful to watch, the ground brown beans, bubbling and rising, volcanic, always somehow unexpected and triumphant . . .

Standing at the counter, I watched the grounds rise. The hot steam tickled my nostrils; Sneff sneff, I thought, thinking of the protagonist of David Lynch's Blue Velvet, of which I'd only seen the first half and which I had hated. Since I didn't have a timer—my old one had broken and I hadn't replaced it—I watched the beans intently; when they stopped rising, I would begin the real pour. I leaned my left hand on the counter and watched as the coffee bloomed comfortingly; I stared into the rising blackness until the tiny elevating bubbles began to look like craters, sinking into themselves, the last of the water having soaked into the grounds; I took a deep breath; I looked around the kitchen.

The elongated spout of my electric kettle, snake-like and sentient-seeming, allowed for a controlled pour; I held my arm up, elbow slightly higher than my shoulder, bent at a ninety-degree angle, and poured in a clockwise motion, starting with small circles in the center, then moving out until I was at the edge; then I poured myself back into the center, pausing briefly when the water level rose too high. The liquid trickled thinly from the filter down into the glass.

The sound of the brown liquid dripping pleased me; it reminded me of something. I stood at the counter, kettle in hand, a slight rush of goosebumps on my arm, like a breeze; I poured more circles and stared into the blackness.

The coffee dripping sounded exactly like Violet peeing. Violet's pee seemed to slap more gently against the toilet water than mine (that is, when I aimed for the center of the bowl; I often peed on the walls of the bowl to prevent what I viewed as an obscene noise from occurring—my urine pounding water, sounding almost like a kind of guzzling—at which times mine would be less audible than hers). I felt self-conscious that, to a woman who had overheard the pee streams of various men, mine would sound weaker comparatively, something a discerning mind might logically conclude was correlated to smaller penis size. Even though Violet had seen my penis countless times, I still didn't want to give anything away; I didn't want the strength of my stream to factor into her attraction toward me— and how could it not?

On good days, I confidently aimed at the center of the bowl and let my sound resound throughout the bathroom. There was something rather special about being able to aim; Violet could not. This made me feel better about myself: for all of the ways in which women were better than men, we would always have our ability to pee on things. I recalled, as the coffee pattered through and I kept pouring, an essay I'd read in which the author called the male pee stream an "arc of transcendence." Freud said that ancient man used to show off for his female counterpart by putting out fires with his pee—something ancient woman could not do. But woman was complete, according to this essay, physically and psychologically; a symbolic mystery (due to her comparatively hidden genitalia); the devouring force from which all life came; though also an *earthbound squatter*, whereas men had external genitals which they must learn to aim and with which they must project. From this initial metaphor of male genitalia, the essay claimed, all of culture, science, philosophy, math—all of civilization—*sprung*.

Throughout my own history of peeing, I'd wanted to be silent, or the loudest, depending on my mood. Though even when I peed stealthily on the side of the bowl, it was ultimately because I wanted to be the loudest: by removing myself from the competition, as it were, I ensured that Violet couldn't judge my performance and rank me in her pee-strength hierarchy.

In the past, due to opioids, I would often have to stand in front of the bowl for inappropriately long stretches, waiting for the liquid to flow forth, oozing slowly like squeezed sludge through the tube to my tip, like something thick. I absurdly considered that perhaps, to throw off the suspicion of those around me, I should pee on the side of the bowl. If no one ever heard anything, they may be less suspicious.

I remembered once having to pee before a reading at a so-called communist art gallery in

Ohio. I stood in front of the toilet for what must have been ten minutes, coming so close to peeing several times, but inevitably getting distracted, the pee slinking back into wherever it came from, people knocking on the door in line. I came out without peeing, then decided not to use the allotted microphone during my reading, instead sitting on one of the giant PA speakers and rocking back and forth, reading while having to pee. No one could hear my voice and the reading went terribly.

Standing at the counter, making coffee, I remembered the gallerist there, his round face, beady eyes set back in his head, when my memory was interrupted by my arm, which faintly ached; I shook it a few times, then resumed pouring water, enchanted once more by the pleasing trickle of the coffee.

People were different, I knew; Violet and I were certainly different—but in this way? It was not always best to extrapolate from experience. I lazily attempted to draw into my mind specific memories of hearing Violet pee, and compared them with memories, which I willed myself to conjure, of hearing other people pee. I remembered, or imagined remembering, listening to my first girlfriend pee in the bathroom off her parents' kitchen, then imagined, in the space of less than one second, wiping my hands on the bright yellow shower curtain in that same bathroom. Pee . . . I thought, trying to focus. I imagined hearing my most recent ex-girlfriend pee—our bathroom was also off the kitchen—but conceded reluctantly that I could access no such memory.

Regrouping and preparing, as I sometimes did, suddenly and apropos of nothing, for an imaginary future argument in which I would have to defend myself for the thoughts I was having, I felt preemptively defensive; I recalled a night when the communist art gallerist, whose face appeared to me now like a vision, had asked me, rather aggressively, over tacos, why I liked Jordan Castro, whom we'd been discussing, and about whom the gallerist had been making abstract and aggressive claims. "Why would he write the things he writes," the gallerist asked, accusatorially, "unless he wants to return to a state of oppressive . . ." I'd blocked out everything after the word "oppressive" and grinned down at my tacos. After he was done, and much to my embarrassment, I replied weakly, "I don't . . . know what Jordan Castro wants. I think he writes fiction."

After a pause, the communist gallerist asked, rather snarkily, if I would "go so far" as to say that Jordan Castro's "*body-fascist* novel" was "just fiction." Shaken by the feverishness of my inquisitor, I'd smiled even wider at my tacos, and replied, simply, "Yes."

The narrator of one of Jordan Castro's novels was an amateur bodybuilder, and the novel, due to its being released while the culture was having a "reckoning with toxic masculinity," was received harshly by many, who described it variously as "fascist," "protofascist," "fatphobic," or, curiously, "not what we need right now." In a matter of weeks, reviews had been written with titles such as "We Read Jordan Castro's Body Novel, So You Don't Have To" and "Jordan Castro's Fitness Privilege," which dealt not so much with the book's literary qualities as with the effect it might have in reality, due to supposed hidden meanings in some of the sentences. Many on Twitter, who had not read the book, began to ascribe certain qualities not just to the narrator but to Jordan Castro himself, such that the difference between Jordan Castro and his narrator were flattened into an indistinguishable sameness, composed of troublingly contagious abstractions. Quotes from the novel circulated online, as if he had said them himself, and half-quotes circulated too, cut off at points that, had the whole quote been included, would have completely negated the part that was shared.

I, like the communist gallerist, had believed what I'd seen, or rather glimpsed, of these controversies, not having looked into them myself, but understanding, through my vague online engagement with some writers who were particularly upset, that Jordan Castro was a reactionary, or a crypto-reactionary, that his novels weren't novels but dangerous weapons, written with secret motivations, and that this was the consensus among good, learned people.

Once one accusation was leveled, it spread, and many more snowballed, in a kind of mimetic avalanche, until people were tweeting about things other people had said, or things his characters had said, even in jest, attributing these words uncritically to Castro. His novel about weightlifting was no longer a satire about the Nietzschean response to a weakening culture, but a *reassertion of patriarchal values and aesthetics*; one semi-viral tweet even accused him of "wanting the government to force everybody to stay below a certain body fat percentage" because one of his characters had jokingly suggested it; and his newest novel—the one that was in the mail on its way to me, a first person narrative about drug addiction—had already been rejected by one of the literary media as promoting *the dangerous idea that anyone can overcome addiction, when the truth was that not everyone could.*

These misunderstandings were then used as dots in what was essentially a map—other dots included his past books, things he'd said in interviews, and so on—onto which people drew straight, connecting lines, creating a pattern out of disparate half-quotes, misquotes, and so on, then solidifying this pattern as the defining characteristic of Castro's work, usually reducing it to one or two words, and creating a kind of dogma which, if a reader even so much as cast doubt on it, called into question that reader's own moral integrity, and often turned the anger toward him.

Castro was not the only one this kind of thing had happened to, and at some point, perhaps out of boredom, or morbid curiosity, or perhaps because I'd realized that I hadn't actually read any of his work, every time I saw one of these shitstorms taking place, I made a conscious decision to engage directly with the source material. This is what led me to read the initial conversation between Castro and the art historian, and to, eventually, become a fan of Jordan Castro.

I visualized my dinner opponent, the communist gallerist, and, standing at the counter, began arguing against him again in my head. I tried to remember, like scrolling quickly through an online database, a quote by Jordan Castro about his artistic goals, or any interview I'd read with him, that I could paraphrase from memory and that specifically addressed the communist gallerist's question—accusation, really—but couldn't think of anything.

I floundered momentarily while organizing my thoughts. At the dinner, I'd pretended not to know what the communist gallerist was asking about, but I knew that he'd initially been asking about Jordan Castro's first novel, which critics had said contained only one flat female character— the narrator's girlfriend—and some other female appearances as, more or less, objects. Reviewers had attributed certain worldviews to Jordan Castro—none of which he'd claimed, and all of which he'd explicitly refuted—because of his fiction, and people, like the communist gallerist, took issue with him because of that. They didn't think the world portrayed in Castro's work, or the thoughts his narrators experienced, were how they ought to be.

I imagined the communist gallerist's face, round, though admittedly handsome (however, the unfortunate fact of his personality and worldview rendered even his good looks off-putting), and wanted nothing more than to go back in time and dominate him. He had brought up, then disavowed, *human nature* too: "There is no such thing as *human nature*," he'd said, using that phrase, "human nature," like a middle schooler, and I imagined myself at that dinner, again, articulating myself much better than I had then.

If we have a nature, I thought hesitantly. If we have a nature, then we must contend with it, otherwise whatever we are trying to do won't work. I recognized the phrase "contend with" not as mine, but as Jordan Castro's. If we aren't just computers, created with blank software, downloading and running different programs as society dictates, but rather human beings with a complicatedly multifaceted biological, psychological, historical, even spiritual nature, which evolved over millennia—and are also, in part, socially constructed—then any ideology that doesn't take into account all of those things will inevitably lead to dystopia. Murderous dystopia . . . I thought, pouring water onto coffee grounds; I recognized "murderous" as not my own either. *Murderous?* I imagined my dinner opponent, the communist gallerist, mocking me, and realized I was actually remembering when another friend, Eric, during a different argument over a different meal, had exasperatedly repeated the word "*Murderous?*" back to me after I'd said that the idea of population control was fundamentally "murderous," a word that I immediately wished I hadn't used, and which I'd made a mental note of then to never use again.

Jordan Castro . . . I thought, quoting myself from the dinner with the communist gallerist, trying to discern where things went wrong. I visualized myself grinning feebly at my plate; I've often played it over in my head, thinking, at times, that I might have seemed confidently smug—none of us knew what Jordan Castro wanted, and he did write fiction, that was obviously true—while simultaneously reserved, as if my dinner opponent's suggestion was so patently absurd that it warranted little engagement; but other times, viewing it more as I'd experienced it in real time, I recalled myself as having seemed sheepishly avoidant. I yearned to go back in time and vanquish him, the communist gallerist, with new information, a more developed worldview, and a levelheaded willingness to engage in confrontation. Standing at the counter, I consoled myself: what I'd said was fine; it was he who had been belligerent, and who had been belligerent the entire evening, constantly rambling about things like how *milk was a big win* for the *American Left*, and how if art didn't challenge this or that power, it *wasn't punk*; then later, stumbling loudly into our friend's living room where we had all fallen asleep soundly, flopping down, and unleashing the worst snores I'd ever had the misfortune of waking up to hear (I was told later this was due to a large metal rod that had been implanted in his spine).

After I had poured the coffee from the Chemex into the mug—a solid stream, akin to my pee when I aimed for the center of the bowl—and had taken my coffee to the table to work on my novel, I thought of Violet sleeping in the other room, and it occurred to me that I had never been in the same room with Violet while she peed. The difference in sound might not be due to stream strength, I considered, but rather to the simple fact that there was a door and walls between us. Though the walls in our house were thin, the mere fact of the sound passing through solid material would be enough to change the tone; things always sounded different when you were on the other side of them. I raised the mug to my lips and sipped gingerly, inhaling a spurt of air with the coffee, perceiving myself in that moment as "looking like a douche," aware that my pinky was extended, testing the temperature before fully indulging.

I touched my laptop and the screen lit up; I logged in and opened the internet; particles of coffee sunk into the back of my damp tongue and the roof of my mouth; I delighted in the taste and temperature. I took another sip—then unthinkingly took out my phone and opened Instagram. I closed Instagram and put my phone next to my laptop, shuffling it side to side and then picking it up an inch off the table and dropping it. I shuffled it twice more, then moved my hands toward the keyboard and typed "doc" in the search bar, opening my novel.

I read the first few sentences while sipping coffee. They were completely fucking terrible. The sentences didn't follow one another, they didn't sound good, and they weren't interesting. I looked away from my laptop toward the living room; my chest felt like somebody was stepping on it, or like water was flooding my lungs. I opened Twitter and read a few tweets, didn't comprehend anything, then closed Twitter and looked at my novel with unfocused eyes. I opened a new tab and clicked Twitter again; I picked up my phone then put it down.

My body felt at once empty and full; my neck felt weak, like it might crumple under the weight of my head, leaving me with no neck. I couldn't get anything done. I felt hopelessly at the mercy of Twitter; I scrolled while feeling numbly doomed. This was my life. I took a small sip of coffee.

I wanted to click out of Twitter and work on my novel, but couldn't activate my limbs; I imagined myself screaming *arrrrrggggghhhhh*, picking up my laptop and throwing it at the wall, sparks flying, my imaginary gigantic muscles pulsing; an ad caught my eye—I mistook it for a picture of a dog, when in reality it was a picture of a bottle—and I continued scrolling Twitter, using only, it seemed, part of my consciousness, or using only my body, while my imagination struggled to free itself from the grip of some other, dark force.

A large part of me felt turned off, or elsewhere.

This was not a problem specific to this moment or morning; I had been fragmenting in this manner for years. The cumulative amount of time I spent unintentionally scrolling through feeds, looking at things I was more thrust into than chose, was unfathomable. I literally couldn't think about it. It felt as if Twitter was taking part of my consciousness from me, sucking it out of wherever it was, and fuzzily disrupting it, like an energy field, not a website, moving through the air toward me, while simultaneously pulling me outside of myself and "into" Twitter, fusing the two in midair. This could actually be the case, I considered. Was consciousness a product of my brain, like I imagined? Or was it something outside of my brain that my brain "tapped into"—something that also contained Twitter?

While I read a book, text seemed to enter my brain through my eyes, then from there into somewhere in my psyche, but with Twitter, the tweets seemed to enter straight into my body. I scrolled Twitter, "reading" tweets, while half-thinking about other things, focusing on the tweets for varying lengths of time (deciseconds, seconds, one or two minutes), then having no thoughts, or at least no thoughts I could remember or experience as thoughts; all while feeling low-level anxiety about not wanting to be on Twitter in the first place. Sometimes twenty or thirty minutes would pass and I'd have no recollection of what I had looked at or thought about. I never clicked Twitter because I wanted to read tweets, and I never felt grateful for having clicked it; I never felt enriched, or fulfilled, or more knowledgeable; I clicked Twitter most often like a stress response.

I looked at the time—9:31 a.m. I closed Twitter. I picked up my phone and opened Instagram; I saw a picture of a porcelain dunce cap on a porcelain stool, and I tapped the screen twice with my thumb—a large white heart appeared then disappeared on the picture; a small white heart beneath the bottom left-hand corner of the picture turned red. I began watching the stories in my queue: a picture of a black-and-white cat in bushes; a picture of two cats near the same bushes; a picture of three different cats in tall grass; a bag of croutons; a turquoise-colored wine bottle opener with a GIF of the Nintendo character Princess Peach, with her arms spread out like Christ, spinning in circles, superimposed on the photo; an incomprehensible image with the text "#FOOTBUBBLES" superimposed on it; a video of a street with the text "One of our neighborhood kitties died here because of speeding and reckless driving. Slow down buddies."; a video of a football video game on a TV, in which the person filming kept saying, "Excuse me," each time the player with the ball successfully dodged the players trying to tackle him; a video of an obese man leaning against a counter in a recording studio with loud rap music playing, the bared-teeth emoji superimposed on it; a video of the rapper Gunna sitting on a couch showing his diamond-studded watch, necklaces, and rings to the camera; a picture of a Russian American podcaster wearing only a shirt that said "BUILD THE WALL, I'll have sex with it" with a picture of Tweety Bird leaning against a brick wall; a picture of a shirt, reposted from another podcaster, that said "The Weedpranos / Smoke weedaboutit" with a picture of the main characters from *The Sopranos* on it. I double-clicked the circle button at the bottom of my phone and swiped up, exiting Instagram. I sipped my coffee.

My novel, I thought, suddenly, albeit cautiously, determined. I tried to think of something empowering that would make me focus on my novel, but couldn't. Do it, I thought. Just do it.

I felt fleetingly, decisively empowered by the simple, direct sentiment, until I realized—first by sensing something was off, then by articulated thought—that it was the Nike slogan.

Just do it, I thought again, trying nevertheless to convince myself of its power. Just . . . I felt weak. I sipped my coffee while picking up my phone and opening Instagram.

Maybe I just needed to stop trying to force it, I considered. If I allowed myself to relax and drink coffee, then I would get all of my social media use out of my system; I would relax and indulge myself, while also becoming energized by the coffee, then get a lot of work done on my novel afterward. I sipped my coffee, then put my mug down on the table. I scrolled past the porcelain dunce cap again; past a short video of a small dog running through a hallway; an advertisement for Ice Breakers mints; a picture of my friend, playing a harp in the woods, naked; past a picture of a pile of Klonopin in a pair of women's underwear next to some flower petals; a picture of five or so fake watermelons. I paused at a picture of text that Eric had posted.

"Some of my friends have kids and i support them and love their kids so much," the post began, "but i wanted to take this opportunity to say that if any of my friends have kids from now on i will not support them and we will stop being friends. i just want to be clear. Again i love all the already existing kids, there just shouldn't be anymore from now on. I love kids so much, this is a perfect number of kids."

Eric . . . I thought, looking at the post. Juvenile.

"Juvenile" wasn't a word I thought often, and I felt surprised by it, while at the same time remembering—in faint images which occurred alongside my more dominant cognitive sensations—the rapper Juvenile. Seven people had liked Eric's post; I clicked to see the list and didn't recognize any of the names; I felt like the post was directed at me.

Eric and I had, a year or so ago, gotten into a somewhat stunted argument about having kids; it wouldn't have been the first time Eric posted something snarky after we'd had a disagreement. In the past, I'd emailed him, offering to talk, but he never wanted to talk, and the last time—when he'd tweeted something about hating people who liked Jordan Castro—he hadn't even responded to my email.

I met Eric in 2011 through mutual friends in New York, who had introduced us because he had just published a novel and I was working on a novel (which never came out), and we'd become close over the years. We'd bonded over a shared ironic disposition toward the world, an unarticulated hatred toward almost everything; we wanted the same things, were afraid of the same things, and looked up to the same people. At a time when everything had seemed hostile and opposed to me, Eric had been dynamic and fun—a kind of confidant amidst the stupid, brutal world; and unlike the predictable violence of interacting with others, who were always smiling and saying predictable things, spending time with Eric often surprised me. I'd felt less alone, when we would stand in the back at literary events, scoffing; or listen to rap music, talking shit, free-associating. In short, I was critical of everything, because I was afraid of everything, and Eric was, too: we were doubles, confirming for each other what each already knew. Our lives continued to progress in similar directions, and we grew more and more the same: my best friend died shortly before Eric's best friend died; I'd started writing again after a break and Eric had started writing again after a break; I'd gotten sober around the time Eric had decided to stop drinking and start taking psychedelics. Eric and I had joked that we were "fused," a word which he had gleaned from a hat he had that said, in a font that was not dissimilar to the Florida mug, "FUSION," and so I'd come to think of my years being friends with Eric as *the fusion years*. Strangely enough, it was shortly after Eric's *fused observation* that we started to conflict.

I thought of Eric's novel, distantly desiring to work on my own novel, and felt a pang of disdain toward Eric's novel, then my own novel— then projected my disdain outward toward the literary world, at least the part of it that I could see online. Eric's novel's protagonist, based on himself, meandered through his life in New York City; he went from place to place, had this or that thought, was in this or that mood. It was a fundamentally lifeless book. Critics had celebrated the novel's critique of privilege, the way it showed the emptiness of privilege; one reviewer even referenced the "dunce-like quality" of "a privileged life" as portrayed in Eric's novel. This was what the literary world did now, I'd reminded myself, they celebrated stupid novels for stupid reasons. Every novel, like Eric's novel, failed as a novel, but since no one wanted to read novels, no one noticed, and instead of despairing over the failed state of our literary culture, they rejoiced, like madmen delirious from bashing their heads into the wall. Eric's novel was one such wall. Every review focused on something other than its novelistic qualities: it was a political, historical, or sociological document; it was a philosophical treatise, and so on. What was the point of literature, I'd wondered, if it could only ever be something else?

I looked at Eric's post again. Eric, I thought dismissively, feeling my heart rate increase, scanning the words on the screen: "this is the perfect number of kids." What an incomprehensible sentiment, an utterly incomprehensible sentiment. I imagined Eric twitching and mumbling, "perfect number of kids," and came to a simple conclusion—Eric is a moron. I'd heard these kinds of confused, frankly moronic sentiments from Eric before, and there was a time in my life—predominantly during the fusion years—when I would have agreed with them; but now, I considered, sitting at my kitchen table, I felt disturbed by Eric's nonsensical moronism.

I scrolled down a little, quickly passed pictures I didn't quite see, then scrolled up to Eric's post. The reasons Eric was against having children were all, ironically, childish, I thought. There were childish pseudo-environmentalist, pseudo-humanitarian, pseudo-egalitarian reasons for not having children—for everything really—and Eric's child aversion was some soupy combination of all three. Of course, it was really just nihilism; everything with people like Eric was nihilism; and as a result of this nihilism Eric was unable to see, or understand, the value of life enough to want to perpetuate it. The perfect number of kids . . . I thought. Since when did Eric stop being a novelist and become the perfect-number-of-kids decider?

I recalled the argument I'd had with Eric during which I'd regrettably used the word "murderous" and had asked him why—especially if, as he claimed, he thought "voluntary extinction" was the only "ethical solution" (to what problem, he didn't clearly articulate)—he didn't kill himself. This was, after all, the logical conclusion of his worldview. The only reason he didn't kill himself, according to him, was because he was "selfish." It didn't occur to me until later, though I wish it had sooner, I thought, that while all Eric knows of himself is that he is selfish, that is not all he is. Eric only thinks he understands one of the reasons he hasn't killed himself, but in reality Eric doesn't kill himself for many reasons; the only one he lets himself see is that he is selfish, because if he were to admit anything else, his *perfect number of kids* worldview would become absurd. If Eric were to admit that he thought that any aspect of life was good, and honestly thought about the implications of that, he would be forced to contend with the resultant responsibility and risk—Eric would have to change.

The gist of his argument, I recalled unhappily, was that people—especially first world people—use a lot of resources. You shouldn't bring a baby into this world, he said, airily drawing out syllables and pausing too long between words, because of how many people are starving and suffering. He paused, I recalled, to take a dramatic sip from his iced tea, then bit into his cheese omelette, before continuing with a mouth full of food. It is wrong to bring a new person into this world when there is so much pain in it already, he'd said, especially when that pain is unevenly distributed. And besides, he'd said, any new baby will suffer too. It is not right to cause suffering.

Wow. Eric has always been a belligerent narcissist, I thought, sitting at my kitchen table. The only reason Eric thinks inequality and suffering are the most important things is because he doesn't know anything; and the only reason he thinks more people would cause more harm is because he fundamentally hates people. Eric's worldview, I thought, if our diner conversation was any indication, is based on his self-centered perception of a very small portion of media about a very small portion of history, and because that small portion of history is unprecedentedly wealthy and peaceful, Eric is spoiled and ignorant.

I sipped my coffee and stared blankly at the wall in front of me; I furrowed my brow. I narrated my thoughts to myself in full sentences, imagining arguing with Eric.

First world people hurt the environment, I thought, mimicking Eric. Eric's kid aversion had nothing to do with the environment, and everything to do with himself, I thought. Eric didn't know anything about the environment. He lived in New York City and never spent any time in nature; looking at his life, one could only come to the conclusion that Eric, aside from occasionally lazing around on the beach, hated nature, and did everything in his power to sequester himself from it and destroy it. Eric spent his life ruining every relationship he had, thinking only of himself, drinking and doing drugs, and hurting people; this had more to do with Eric's kid aversion than anything else. I impulsively opened Google Docs in a new tab and began typing furiously.

One way of discerning people's intentions, I typed, is to look at the outcomes of their actions. When there is an egregious discrepancy between what we say and what we do, what we say we believe and how we live, there is no reason to believe our explanations. Eric, like so many writers of our time, I typed, exists in his imagination, but when he is confronted with another, with anything external to him, he crumbles, and so he lashes out and blames the world for not conforming to his own malformed ideas. This is why there is *the perfect number of kids*; this is why human life should have no future.

Eric is a narcissist, I typed, imagining Eric

in his fusion hat. Eric is an impotent narcissist, I typed.

I sipped my coffee, picked my phone up off the table, and glimpsed my reflection in the blackness of the screen; then I pressed the circle button at the bottom of my phone, typed in my password, and looked at Eric's Instagram post. I could still see my reflection on the screen, and I surveyed the general shape of my head as I sipped another small sip of coffee and suddenly felt an exhilarating burst of energy: I could start a new novel! I looked at what I'd written about Eric. I could write a novel where I just talked shit about Eric; I could write my own version of *Woodcutters*.

Woodcutters by Thomas Bernhard was one of my favorite novels; a contemporary *Woodcutters* would be sweet, I considered. I feverishly glanced at Eric's post on my phone, then, right leg bouncing on the ball of my foot, turned my attention to my laptop.

The last time I went to New York and saw Eric he told me that he "can't read anymore," I typed, my face breaking into a grin. I imagined Eric with a dumbfounded expression, struggling to discern literal meanings of words in a book beneath a lamp in an otherwise pitch-dark room. Kill police, I thought, amusedly, suddenly remembering the drawing on his wall that said "Kill police."

Eric has always had a problem with authority, I typed. Eric has always felt that authority was an affront to him personally, and was based on nothing more than arbitrary power. For Eric, everything is about power, I typed, because Eric craves power more than anything. Eric hates policemen, parents, teachers, even firemen, all with the same indiscriminate zeal. Eric hates philosophy, science, religion, and art, I continued. Even though Eric has taught countless classes, and even though Eric has taken more classes than me, Eric hates school, and he hates education; he hates the very nature of learning because in order to learn something new he would have to admit he didn't know something, and would have to defer to people from the past. Eric, like so many of our literary vandals, I typed, has only ever read with a red pen in his hand. And even though he pretends to believe he doesn't know everything—he might even say he doesn't know anything—nothing about his behavior indicates that he believes it. Eric belligerently denies the value of anything he can't understand—especially if it has perceived power across a dimension he thinks is important—and he belligerently insists, through his actions, which are so far from his words as to seem like they come from two separate people, that he is right about everything.

Eric acts like he is right about everything, when in fact, he is wrong about everything.

I felt excited at the prospect of writing a novel like *Woodcutters*. I would talk shit about Eric and everyone else I felt unarticulated aversion toward, while inveighing against a certain worldview which had been infecting my peers like an intellectual plague. This plague spread on social media and throughout the universities and its symptoms included an inability to think deeply, speak honestly, or interact with anyone or any idea that tried to resist said plague, resulting in what seemed like severe brain damage, among other things. *Woodcutters* . . . I thought, sipping my coffee. Ah, yes—my *Woodcutters*. Bernhard had employed repetition to achieve a certain rhythmic, hypnotic effect, and I could do that too, I considered in the form of a single-word thought: Repetition. I looked at what I'd typed and decided not to think about line breaks or style—I didn't want to lose momentum. I read what I had written so far and picked up where I had left off.

Eric is dismissive of anything counterintuitive, of anything paradoxical, of anything requiring real effort, I wrote. He is afraid, and egotistical, and lazy. Eric is afraid—I deleted "Eric is afraid," then moved my hands away from the keyboard and sighed, looking at the small mass of text on the screen. I already felt accomplished. Repetition, I thought, like a languishing octopus weakly unfurling its tentacles. No, I admonished myself, aware that I had just one second ago resolved to not think about style.

Eric is a narcissist, I typed. Eric, having had some success as a young novelist, but not as much success as he had hoped, and not the kind he had anticipated, let it get to his head, and then it crumpled him, I typed. Eric, having had some success, but not enough success, was crumpled like a sock by the success amount, I typed. In his head, I continued, Eric had soared to the highest of heights, but when he encountered reality, he'd spiraled to the lowest depths, hating the world for not confirming his conception of himself, which he could only nurse, like a wound, while alone, or on drugs.

And so instead of changing, I typed, he crumpled, which is to say he stayed essentially the same.

There came a moment in every artist's life, I typed, when, confronted with the defense mechanism of his work thus far, he moved through whatever he was hiding from and changed, or ran away and spiraled further into the delusion. Eric, following our literary culture, chose to spiral, picking apart the meaning of words like "confronted" and "with" and "defense mechanism" until he was paralyzed by nothingness; then, in the end, to fill the void, he became a mindless ideologue.

There were many such cases, I considered, as I abstractly thought about those who in our literary culture fetishized the void, or sought to fill it with fulfillment of unbridled desire. The majority, however, I considered, sought to fill it with the sand of ideology. I thought of Eric's ex-girlfriend, who he'd dated for three months one winter, and who seemed to change him permanently, for the worse. She was much younger than him, and the only thing I knew about her, besides the fact that she went to Oberlin, was that his mouth became dry when he kissed her.

Ever since Eric dated that young Oberlin graduate he's been different, I typed. Eric's brand of nihilism has been different ever since he dated that young girl who went to Oberlin. Whereas before, Eric hated everything and everyone and lashed out against them all indiscriminately, now Eric only hated people he could categorically justify hating through the lens of his young liberal arts school ex-girlfriend. It was as if he hadn't acquired a girlfriend, but a pair of glasses, and instead of dating her, Eric wrapped her around his face and now saw everything through her. Eric's ex-girlfriend taught him the *new meanings* of words like "racism," "patriarchy," "privilege," and so on, and so Eric used these *new meanings* to become even more of an asshole. Eric still hates everything and everyone, I typed, only now he has a mechanism for justifying it and feeling morally superior because of it, and since Eric has always included himself among the people he's hated, his new Oberlin-graduate nihilism was doubly attractive: Eric got to act out his resentment while also hating himself, really love-hating himself, and he got to do it while masquerading as a warrior for the less fortunate!

Eric thinks, I typed, that with his haphazard

ideology, he can end certain kinds of suffering, but since Eric has never actually learned anything, the likelihood that he could change anything for the better, even with the best intentions, seems—to put it nicely—low. I pictured Eric's face and hair. Eric is a greasy nincompoop! I surprised myself, grinning. Eric is a greasy-weasy nincompoop! I typed.

I deleted "Eric is a greasy-weasy nincompoop!" while grinning.

Eric doesn't want his friends to have kids, for the sake of other, less fortunate kids, I typed, appalled. I recalled some Max Scheler I'd read, in which he wrote about the shift from "love thy neighbor" to "love mankind"; the shift, for Scheler, was a violent one, born of suppressed envy. It was difficult, but possible, to love a specific, individual person; but it was literally impossible to love "mankind." One could "love mankind" while hating every real person he knew. One could "love the environment" and do the same. The move from loving real people to "loving" abstractions was in reality a shift from love to hate. Eric did not love mankind; Eric simply hated his neighbor. He did not love "kids"; he simply hated kids and didn't want any more of them to exist.

Eric, following his liberal arts school ex-girlfriend, was so full of impotent hatred for the people in his life that he had no choice but to love "the less fortunate"; then he could use "the less fortunate" as a new bat to beat people over the head with, as opposed to his old bat of pure nihilism.

My teeth clicked against each other and I thought about how, in this moment, it was perhaps not my love of kids, or life, but my feelings toward Eric that were animating me—I felt drawn in and possessed by some mimetic rivalry—but I forcefully banished this thought to a part of my mind that did not have the power to stop my fingers from typing: I was, after all, accomplishing something; I was working.

Ever since Eric's Oberlin infusion, I continued, of ketamine and hand-me-down theory, Eric thinks he has changed, when really he has just changed the bat with which he beats people over the head.

Yes, I considered, satisfied. I was finally working.

I envisioned Eric with a tiny bat, bonking people on the head, his weak arms not generating enough force to hurt, but annoying nonetheless, and I considered my teenage political phase, reading Marx and Emma Goldman, riding my bike to school, dumpster diving for donuts, lecturing my friends and girlfriends about capitalism, playing in punk bands.

Some people, people like Eric, I typed, envisioning my younger self, rejected life the moment they were born. Political opinions, for people like Eric, are born less from a desire to help, and more from an innate need to lash out against something (or in Eric's case, everything). First, Eric lashed out at his parents; then, Eric lashed out at the world; then Eric lashed out at his friends; then, finally, Eric lashed out at me. Eric has been throwing one big temper tantrum ever since he was sixteen, I typed. Now, all of a sudden, he is a moral person who knows what's right and wrong and good and bad for everyone!

It felt good to be typing. It felt like how I'd imagined journaling to feel, but I wasn't journaling—I was writing a novel. Finally, I was writing a novel. I thought about eventually publishing my new novel and immediately, bizarrely, began evaluating my earning potential if my *Woodcutters* novel didn't sell and I couldn't find a good job in academia, something I wasn't remotely on track to do—I didn't even have a bachelor's degree—but about which I occasionally fantasized. I stared blankly away from the screen, wondering what I was going to do as a career, especially since my *Woodcutters* novel would invariably not sell. Would I finish my BA, then go to grad school? Find another job? I bleakly defaulted to romanticizing a manual labor job—at least on a construction crew there would be no bureaucratic ghouls, and my coworkers wouldn't care about my *Woodcutters* novel—before reminding myself that I hated working jobs like that: when I'd worked as a laborer on a crew framing houses after initially getting sober, I'd fantasized about pretending to slip on the ice and falling down the elevator shaft every day.

Violet wanted children though, and I wanted children too, so I would need a well-paying job to support, or at least contribute substantially to, our future family. Unless my *Woodcutters* novel established me as a bestselling author, which seemed unlikely, I would need to find something consistent to do for a living. I resented my position in life, and wished that I had made better decisions. The amount of work I had cut out for me manifested as an actual weight on my shoulders, and the caffeine seemed to beeline straight to it—soaking into, zapping, then paralyzing my muscles—adding to the tension, as I sighed and sipped my coffee, resolving to write more about Eric.

It is scary, I typed, for people, as they get older, to think that maybe they have chosen the wrong path in life. So much would have to change in order for Eric to have a kid successfully. How much of what Eric views as a moral position is actually post hoc justification for a less-than-desirable position in life? Eric doesn't have the ability to make a lot of money, and he thinks being rich is immoral; Eric is physically weak, and he thinks it's always wrong to have the capacity for violence; Eric is too emotionally stunted to care for a child and he thinks it's wrong to have children. I thought about how Eric, after getting rejected from an independent press which was funded by a billionaire heiress, began attacking authors who had been published by the press on Twitter; how he had had a "change of heart" and now "cared about things," he'd tweeted, impotently harassing people online.

I typed a bit more forcefully, then paused to sip my coffee. I felt clever and good. Eric doesn't have thoughts, I typed, but sentiments. Eric is a sentimentalist, I typed.

Some near thoughts moved through my head as I pressed the return key twice. I wanted to try to type more about the connection between Eric's *perfect number of kids*, his Oberlin infusion, and his life hatred. Eric has always fundamentally rejected life, I typed, because he has always fundamentally rejected the fact of suffering. Eric, who hates to suffer, has always fundamentally rejected it, and the entirety of his so-called worldview, which is really just a hodgepodge of sentiments, is a reaction against suffering.

I sighed and re-centered myself, trying to connect what seemed to be disparate thoughts about Eric; I felt self-conscious about having allowed myself to rant so relatively unselfconsciously; I reminded myself that this was just a draft—my novel would go through many drafts—and that I'd been trying to write all morning, so I should just keep going.

I paused, then continued. The jump from "life is meaningless" to "people should stop procreating" to "the best thing for the world would be for humanity to be wiped off the face of the earth" is actually rather natural. There is in fact nothing more natural than the move from nihilist to ideologue: they are both narrow-minded and self-centered; they both lead to destruction; and destruction is, in the end, their primary aim.

The only difference between Eric the nihilist and Eric the ideologue is his explanations, I typed. Before, Eric treated his friends and his girlfriends like shit because he was a *bad person*; now he treated them like shit because he was a *good person*. Before, Eric stopped publishing because he was waiting until he wrote something "aesthetically new"; now he wasn't publishing because he wanted to "make space" for other writers, and didn't want to use up unnecessary resources, like paper. Of course, Eric had also been rejected by multiple presses.

Eric's "solution" to every "problem"—a problem that he could never quite specify—always included doing less: he didn't shower, he didn't wash his clothes, he didn't eat, he didn't publish writing, he didn't read, he didn't even think that having children was acceptable for other people. The best thing for the earth, he'd said at the diner, would be for people to stop having kids. The best thing for the earth . . . I thought, in disbelief. Who would be around to say, or care?

My tone had taken on an aggressive quality, but I wasn't feeling angry. I felt less anxious than I had all morning. And though all of this was true of Eric, I had, for much of the time, stopped imagining him specifically while typing. I tried to picture him as vividly as possible now, tilting my head and looking up, to the left.

Eric used to be hot, I typed, beautiful really, but now Eric is ugly.

I picked up my mug, not realizing it was empty, began moving it toward my lips, then stopped short once I saw the white bottom of the mug; I put it down. I'd begun to feel, to some degree, like I was *onto something*, but through the snark and the energy, I guess, it had fizzled away. I looked at my most recent sentences and felt exhilarated: perhaps there had been no such fizzling. I resolved to keep trying. I wiggled my fingers in front of the keyboard and opened and closed my mouth quickly, a twitch I'd had in third grade but had been rid of since childhood.

I paused, remembering, suddenly, an interview Violet and I had recently read in which Jordan Castro dismissively referred to a contemporary author as a "milksop." I looked at my empty mug, pressed the return key twice, and continued.

The nature of life is contingent on suffering, I wrote, suddenly parroting Jordan Castro. To point out that there is suffering, or to point out suffering as a reason for people not to procreate— or as a reason for anything other than the fact that you're alive—is hysterical, I typed. Of course any child brought into this world will suffer, and of course anyone alive now will suffer, and as long as you are alive you will continue to suffer. So what?

I acknowledged that I was almost entirely taking on the tone and worldview of Jordan Castro, but, feeling energized, kept going.

The question is not whether or not one will suffer, I wrote. The question must necessarily be, What will *justify* the suffering? *What will justify suffering?* Evidently, Eric doesn't know. And neither do my peers, I typed. Neither do I! I typed, bizarrely. I shifted my weight onto my right, then left, butt cheek, then re-centered myself and deleted "Neither do I!"

Millennials suffer from the age-old delusion that material conditions of life are the primary cause of suffering, I typed, self-conscious about my uncharacteristically didactic tone and the use of the word "millennial" and the phrase "age-old."

147

Much of human misunderstanding is caused by this delusion, I typed. Eric thinks that the main thrust of history is material, that humans are merely material, but that human suffering—which is largely immaterial—is real, I typed.

The problem is not "pain vs. pleasure" or "suffering vs. happiness," but something more like "pain vs. purpose" or "suffering vs. meaning." Meaning is the arch value, I typed, not suffering.

I was veering into weird territory, and, while I wanted to allow myself to write freely, I was too self-conscious to write in such a grand and self-serious tone. I was also merely parroting Jordan Castro—and poorly. I didn't believe what I was typing. The material conditions of life obviously matter a great deal, I considered. I began deleting my most recent sentence, but then decided, again, to just let myself go.

It is surely not the case that the material conditions of life don't matter, I typed, but past a certain point they don't improve the quality of life at all: otherwise the richest and most powerful people would be the most fulfilled, which is obviously not the case. One needs a way to justify living, and to do that requires a worldview that can withstand suffering and self-consciously transcend material conditions, I typed. This is the power of each individual: something that stupid, unthinking, ignorant, material collectivists like Eric ignore.

The creative potential inside us, our ability to perceive and imagine and transcend, to think and to dream, is what gives us each our own unique potential to experience meaning, I typed. It is from our internal world that the external comes into being, not the other way around.

A strange tonal shift had occurred somewhere along the way as I was typing—it wasn't Woodcutters-like anymore; what I'd just typed, I self-consciously considered, was more akin to Alan Watts, who I thought of, when I was infrequently reminded of him, as Kooky Alan Watts, or, The Kooky Monster—but I went with it, trying to focus in on something true. The material of life will never be able to justify Life, I typed. It is hard to even prove life in material terms. Picture a red bird, I typed, thinking of the French phenomenologist Michel Henry; now picture Life, I typed—you can't.

My head swirled with fragments of books I'd only started reading recently or things I only semi-understood; a part of my recent attempts toward change included reading books that I wasn't immediately drawn to, and that I didn't immediately understand. Jordan Castro's novels had been a kind of entry point; I'd decided to read the nonfiction books he referenced in them, since so much of it was out of my traditional mode; so far I'd primarily read contemporary fiction and some philosophy, as well as some stuff about Eastern religions and myth; but recently I'd read Things Hidden Since the Foundation of the World by René Girard, Sun and Steel by Yukio Mishima, and The Present Age by Søren Kierkegaard. I envisioned the new pile of books on my desk, trying, somehow, to glean some insight from one of them to add to my diatribe, but my mind flitted from my book pile to my novel in progress as my eyes focused on the screen.

Suffering, I thought absently. Suffering is part of what makes life tangible to us, I typed, fearing I was going to veer into something Watts-like again. This is partly why vegetarians eat vegetables but not animals: vegetables have an obvious interest in staying alive—they have evolved certain toxins and hard-to-digest polymers—but because they don't feel pain in a manner we recognize, we don't feel that their life is qualitatively the same as ours. It is whether or not something feels a certain kind of pain that makes its life tangible to us, because a certain kind of pain is what makes our own life tangible to us.

That is another problem with Eric, I typed. He is a vegetarian.

I was getting worked up and off track, and feared I was typing incoherently—though I also felt clear and like I'd been articulating myself well; these feelings oscillated sometimes by the second—so I took a deep breath and shifted the weight between my thighs a few times. Eric . . . I thought, disappointedly. I felt personally attacked and let down. Eric was always subtweeting and passive-aggressively posting about his friends and ex-girlfriends online—how pathetic.

The other day Eric had retweeted a tweet that read "Men are overpaid brainless & self-indulgent w no impulse control / Um, yuck." At first I assumed it was ironic, it was so moronic. What kind of imbecile—besides the kind who is indeed brainless and self-indulgent with no impulse control—would retweet a tweet like that? What kind of self-hating, insecure bullshit was going on with Eric?

Overcome with sudden lethargy, and a

general negative feeling toward what I'd written so far, I pressed the return key twice and typed, "Eric = imbecile, Twitter = insane asylum." I wondered whether or not I was projecting more onto Eric's post than was there, but the coffee seemed to be working, which felt good. It didn't matter whether what I wrote was true about Eric specifically—I was working on my new novel. I knew how quickly the caffeine feeling could turn into pure stress. Any amount of prolonged indecision could paralyze me.

I got up from my chair, grabbed my mug, and made my way toward the counter.

Pouring the last of the coffee from the Chemex into the mug, I felt the edge of the caffeine all at once—my chest was going to explode. Violet hadn't even woken up yet; I was twacked. "Fuck," I said aloud. "Funk," I said, unexpectedly, then smiled. I wiggled my arms out in front of me then moved my arms down to my sides. My chest was in knots; I took my mug back to the table and sat.

I opened the internet and navigated to Gmail, where I typed an email to Li. "Working on a new novel, like *Woodcutters*. Shit-talking Eric," I wrote.

I sent the email and considered the rest of my day. It was 10:03 a.m.; Violet would be up soon. I considered working on my main novel, now that I had finally gotten going, then began lazily lambasting myself with half-formulated insults: I had no idea what I was doing; I had nothing to offer; everything I'd done so far sucked; I didn't have what it took to actually write a good novel; I was a fraud; I would never write anything good; I had never written anything good; I had spent my whole life fucking off delusionally; it would take a lifetime to undo the damage. The shit-talking part of my brain that had only a moment ago been focused on Eric had now turned on me. I looked at the text of my new novel and believed, more than anything, that I would never be able to support a family no matter what I did.

I thought about a few days prior, when, confronted with having to cut the grass, I almost broke down crying. "I'm just the kind of person who cuts the grass now," I'd lamented, my imagined future stretching out before me like a slab of meat.

In moments like that, as in these, I felt, self-indulgently, that it was "too late" for me; that my life consisted and would continue to consist of endless small tasks, shitty tasks, with no over-arching purpose or end. The kinds of things I half-heartedly fantasized about—sustaining a family, a career, a relationship—were just fantasies; I'd wasted too much time conflicted and confused. My choices, over years, had stacked up on top of each other until they felt like external forces, walls that obstructed my view and confined me; even this morning, I considered, I'd made terrible choices unceasingly . . . I couldn't simply become another person.

I heard a small noise in my periphery and felt worried that Violet had woken up and walked into the kitchen, or that she was standing behind me, looking at my laptop. Vvv, I thought, picturing her asleep, then remembering a picture I had taken of her in a white dress, standing on a curved bridge, over a pond.

Fff, I thought. Vvvv. I wished Violet was awake, reading or writing in the living room. I wanted to turn and look at her. I thought about how when Violet was frustrated, she liked to shove her head under my armpit, and I tried to imagine myself, as Violet, squeezing my own head under my armpit, to ease my frustration. I smiled slightly, thinking of her smile, which sometimes "squished" audibly if she did it too fast; due to her lip-to-gum ratio—she had very large gums, something I'd initially felt surprised by and attracted to—air and saliva got "stuck" above her teeth and squished by her moving lips. This "squishy smile" happened when she was un-selfconsciously happy, and I thought that when she woke up I'd try to garner one.

I sighed, tilted my head back over the chair, and closed my eyes. I tried to imagine what our children would be like, but it felt hard to convincingly draw into my consciousness an image. My relationship with Violet was one of my first commitments that felt articulated and good: it was not something based solely on my feelings, which were untrustworthy and inconsistent, but a decision, rooted in love. I tried to imagine what her smile would sound like when she was eighty; it felt easier to imagine being eighty than forty or fifty; there was just so much I didn't know about the future; a part of me wanted to commit to the future—my future—but a part of me felt pulled into myself, into another life that felt less like life, and more like a novel. The desire to live in some kind of articulated way was relatively new for me; I didn't want to be like Eric—this much I knew, at least—but that could easily happen, I considered; I had been like Eric not that long ago. I tried to refocus on this morning, thinking of Violet, then trying to consider my novel, but feeling somewhat torn between the two: when I imagined my future as a novelist, it was often intuitively pitted against my future as a husband, or a father—I imagined myself sitting in a dark room with my laptop forever.

The sound of my pee hitting toilet water sounded like a chip bag crinkling, and it filled my ears as the swirling, apocalyptic thoughts about my novel consumed me. I flushed, tucked my penis back into my pants, put the lid down, then shuffled two steps to my right and stood in front of the mirror, distraught.

My surroundings appeared farther away than they were; everything seemed as if it were in a slightly vibrating cloud; I touched my hair. I walked into the living room and looked at myself in the mirror on the mantle; I puffed my chest, turned sideways, made a face. I feigned looking at the stacks of books on the mantle next to the mirror: fifteen or so *New York Review of Books* titles that I hadn't read; many issues of *NOON*, my favorite literary journal; a clock shaped like a mosque; a certificate for having gone skydiving. I'd been meaning to submit to *NOON* . . . perhaps a section of my novel would work, I considered.

No. No. I recalled my third person present tense novel, feeling, at the mere thought of it, my back muscles tighten and torque, as I considered a scene in which Calvin, the protagonist, wakes in the middle of the night from a dream, dripping with sweat, naked, and disoriented, then sprints into the hallway and projectile shits onto the walls. He falls down the stairs while shitting—"speckles the banister," as it's rendered in the novel—and continues before sitting down on the toilet, spraying the seat with shit and then squishing down into it. Sensing this would not be right for *NOON*, I considered other parts of my novel.

I thought of one part of the novel, a dream, immediately preceding the banister speckling, in which Calvin stands on a small washing machine, telling many small children that he "needs to go away for a while," when suddenly the washing machine starts rumbling and poop bursts into the room from inside it, then shoots in through the windows, shattering glass, rushing in like a flood, the room and everything else spinning and filling with it . . .

It was egregious to include a dream in a third person present tense novel made up largely of flashbacks and fever-induced diarrhea scenes. Though dreams almost certainly had some degree of meaning, they had no place in fiction, which was already dream-like to begin with, and so conveying a dream within a novel was like telling someone about a dream within a dream: it would be nearly impossible to connect with. How many times had someone oppressed me with their dreams, explaining their dream to me in great detail, which, no matter how strange or unexpected, always made me lose interest almost immediately, and which I could not connect with in any meaningful way whatsoever? There was something about dreams that one just forgot. Upon waking, one forgot his own dreams; and upon hearing the dreams of another, one forgot even as the dreamer was still babbling . . .

I felt pulled, or dragged, toward my laptop, as I shuffled half-heartedly in the general direction of my kitchen table, as if to remind myself of something, my novel's tense and point of view perhaps, or something else. I resolved to conquer my negative thoughts by confidently working for a short time—I would simply sit down and start writing, or editing, or discerning what would be good to send to *NOON*, and dispel the bad thoughts; I would only have to focus for fifteen or so minutes; this way, I wouldn't feel the need to distract myself. But, sitting down at my kitchen table, gearing up to work on my novel, I became instantly convinced that the dream scene would be, among other things, too vulgar for *NOON*. The novel was too vulgar in general, even for me; I did not want my first novel to be so vulgar as to not get taken seriously—I was a serious person, who deserved to be taken seriously, and I wanted to have a career.

I opened my laptop and navigated to the Google Doc containing my novel, then scrolled down, absently worrying that if I ever released my novel, I would be committing to a kind of vulgarity that I wouldn't be able to keep up with in the future; I was thinking the phrase—my imagined future nickname—"Vulg Boy" when I encountered the phrase I was looking for: "speckles the banister."

Speckles the banister . . . speckles the banister . . . My skin felt clammy and cold, my body remembering how it had felt when the scene in the novel had taken place in real life; I grinned giddily at the jovial, lilting phrase—*speckles the banister*. The beginnings of goosebumps sprung up on my forearm; I rubbed them, then my laptop, gently; my eyes began to blur as I considered, apprehensively, that I still needed to write the scene in which Calvin walks past his girlfriend the next morning, while she is crying and cleaning the bathroom, before going back to bed and passing out.

Or, no, I had already written it. It was just a few sections below this one. The coffee was making my thoughts feel impossible, like they were words on a screen and my brain was scrolling up and down spastically, or like the screen was freezing then unfreezing unpredictably. I shrunk into my second face, vision blurred, until my skin face felt like it was shivering; my lips hung parted as I imagined my skin face melting, pooling into chunks on the floor, then rising slowly and spinning in the air away from me, laser beams shooting out of my neck. I shook my head to refocus my eyes, but they remained fuzzy; I ran my fingers over the keyboard, not pressing anything, feeling the ridged keys, in a kind of petting motion.

This was a novel based completely on my life, I considered, as I pictured my ex-girlfriend turning toward me, on her hands and knees in the bathroom, asking, too quietly, if I'd "gotten sick." I pictured other things too, but they were abstracted, in half-images that lasted a second or so—doing cocaine and watching interviews with rappers all night in our spare room; lying on our mattress with my phones, confused and alarmed, but also numb and resigned, about the various texts and missed calls; the poster on the bedroom wall illustrating which points in the foot corresponded with which parts of the body; crying in the fetal position while Dillon licked the snot off my face and barked at me.

My memories appeared to me like Instagram stories, flitting past in flattened fragments; I felt them physically in my shoulders and jaw.

I recalled telling people that I was "working on my novel," and then leaving the house, doing drugs in my car, organizing where and when the next shipments of weed and hash oil would arrive, or just lying in bed and watching Netflix. I actually did have a novel I worked on occasionally, but only to ensure that if anyone asked me, I would have something to show them. I fantasized about telling the police that I spent my days writing a novel—I was a novelist—then showing them my "novel" as proof and getting away with whatever crimes they'd accused me of; I would leave it pulled up on my laptop when I suspected my ex-girlfriend might glimpse it; I even told the people I worked with selling weed that the very reason I sold weed was so that I could buy more time to work on my novel.

Sitting at my kitchen table, I tried to remember what this novel—my alibi novel—was about. I knew I'd written it in sentegraphs, and that it was on my old laptop, but that was it. I'd been meaning to get that laptop fixed—it was sitting in a closet at my parents' house, broken—primarily because I had saved a video on it, which I dimly remembered, and wanted to watch, of me counting an enormous pile of money while smoking a cigarette at my kitchen table in Cleveland. That time felt surreally nonexistent to me now. I was sober when I started selling weed, but relapsed at the peak of my activity, often blacking out for many days in a row; and after I came out of the last blackout, I learned that I'd lost $25,000 of my boss's money, given the wrong address to someone else (resulting in his sending $50,000 worth of product to the wrong place), consumed hundreds of pills I'd gotten from one of my underlings, and spent thousands of dollars on an online shopping spree. When I emerged, after projectile shitting, confused and deluded, my laptop wouldn't turn on.

I scrolled to the next fragment in my novel and read a section in which Calvin showers after projectile shitting, then continues shitting in the shower, hunched over and shivering, having trouble staying standing, feverishly considering calling his drug dealer, despite it being 3:30 a.m. He shivers in the hot shower, and slips a little. When Calvin steps out of the shower and towels off, he becomes convinced that his skin is ripping. He is shaking. Seeing that his skin is still intact, he starts to wipe the floor and walls with toilet paper, but everything is moist from the shower steam and the toilet paper keeps ripping. He throws the bunched-up shit-covered pieces of toilet paper in the trash can next to the toilet, and decides to go back to sleep.

Sitting at my kitchen table, highly caffeinated and with a lingering emotional energy left over from my new *Woodcutters* novel, the fact that these scenes had actually happened to me kept re-revealing itself. I'd known it was me, as well as Calvin, who woke after this scene and pooped again, this time into his black Versace boxers as he scuttled toward the bathroom; I'd known it was me, as well as Calvin, who'd then jolted back and forth between his house and outdoor trash can in the January Cleveland cold, trying to dispose of the evidence so his girlfriend wouldn't find out; I'd known it was me, as well as Calvin, to whom all of this had happened, or who had caused all of this to happen, but over time it had begun to feel more like it had happened to Calvin than me, especially when I was sitting in front of my laptop.

"Addiction is a memory disease," I thought suddenly, remembering a line from a memoir by the academic I'd lied to about having copied *Less Than Zero*. Writing fiction is a memory disease, I thought stupidly. Writing my novel had likely changed my memory, though, I considered, since I focused on certain details and didn't include others, then looked at and edited them a lot; I probably accidentally invented details too. One thing I noticed was that instead of remembering myself as having had certain experiences— having "first person memories," as it were—I'd

begun to remember certain things from the perspective of an omniscient other, watching everything happen to "Calvin," who, though he looked
just like me and had done the same things I'd
done, was not me.

Writing about myself in third person allowed
me to take a third-personal view of myself; a view
which eliminated the possibility of choice. One
could not change the past, I thought, reassur-
ingly. It made sense to view one's past in third
person, because one's past was already over. But
then another thought occurred to me, as if from
somewhere outside of myself: one could change
the past. The past is constantly changing, I considered, and this change is entirely dependent
on what happens in the future. The beginning
of a story could mean something entirely different by the end. Life, as well as fiction, was made
up of small, concrete decisions; lived forward,
understood backward; and third person was ultimately a denial of two primary facts of life—
responsibility and choice. Also love, I considered
abstractedly. A third-person person cannot love,
because he cannot choose. Only in the first person, where every choice is simultaneously irrevo-
cable and changeable, can a person love.

I sat at my kitchen table, like a stunned mouse, memory-holing everything I'd just thought, trying to get back to work. I imagined Calvin, not me, snorting Ambien and taking Klonopin and going to speak to a group of recovering addicts about being sober; I imagined Calvin, not me, going back and forth to court every other week, waiting to get prosecuted on my trafficking charge; I imagined Calvin, not me, after the withdrawal had subsided, telling his girlfriend that he'd only taken one pill, and that his plan was to get a job as a car salesman.

Every reader who encountered Calvin could envision their own version of him; filling him with their imagination; whereas I was specific—at least I liked to think so. I remembered an interview with Bret Easton Ellis I'd watched two months after the events in my novel took place, and one month before I'd lied about copying *Less Than Zero*, in which he said that the reason he wrote a sequel to *Less Than Zero* was because he couldn't stop "wondering what the protagonist was up to now." I'd heard other authors talk about their characters this way, like real people, with agency, and many seemed to have considered their entire backstories, even going so far as to mention concrete details about their past that weren't in the text. I recalled that Simone de Beauvoir said that a novel's success was dependent on the illusion of "characterological freedom," and that this freedom was achieved in part because of how the character really seems free to the author, revealing him- or herself line by line, as the author writes. A novel became stale and false when an author tried to confine her characters to a preconceived "type," or a set course of action. What was I doing with Calvin? Did Calvin seem "free"? I thought about Bret Easton Ellis again, thinking, "backstory . . ." and "Bret Easton Ellis." I hadn't even considered "backstory" until now. Would my novel seem even thinner because I hadn't? Backstory, I thought, feeling amused by the simple mashing together of the words "back" and "story."

I touched the trackpad on my laptop and moved the cursor in circles. I opened the Notes app and typed "Calvin: backstory," then deleted ": backstory" and typed "backstory:." I tried to force myself to think.

I remembered being fifteen and unable to sleep, drinking every night alone; rolling around in the grass after high school to try to get the cigarette smell off myself; taking pills weekly, then most days, then every day, then every few hours, until I couldn't do anything without them and needed increasingly harder drugs; growing a goatee; rehabs; the blond drummer in outpatient who'd had a twin who was also addicted to opiates, and who would rack up debt with his dealer then continue to buy drugs, pretending to be his brother; the way everyone in city jail yelled my last name and cheered when I got called for my medication, because my last name sounded similar to that of a man who'd just been in the news for getting caught with three girls chained in his basement; my bunkmate who'd had a seizure and flung his vile-smelling mouth foam all over the cell; the inpatient treatment counselor who lent me *On the Road* by Jack Kerouac because she saw me reading in the smoking area, and the girl who was reading *Lolita*, who I had sex with for months afterward, who had the word "Cocaine" tattooed in cursive on her back.

This last thought distracted me: I envisioned us sitting on my dresser in my bedroom at the halfway house where I lived after rehab, smoking cigarettes and drinking Red Bull, my new belly protruding over the waistband of my boxers. I tried to hold a memory in my mind that I would not write down but that would influence everything else I wrote, something I imagined the reader could intuit—"backstory." I remembered stealing most of the contents of a pill bottle from my friend's dying dad and, when confronted, denying having taken them, then offering to take a drug test if he didn't believe me; going to the store together, buying the drug test, coming up positive for the pills I stole, then continuing to lie. I thought of crawling into my mom's bedroom as she slept, taking $20 out of her purse, which was hidden under her bed, crawling into the hallway, crying, then going back to steal the rest . . .

I scrolled and read some more of my novel, feeling like I was descending a spiral staircase— floating down, like a ghost; intermittently feeling the caffeine swell then stab, rise then shock; I noticed a sentimentality swell and stab with it. I tried to convince myself I was focusing only on the stylistic choices I'd made or should make in my novel by scrunching my eyes and looking closely at certain words.

During the months I'd spent working on my novel, I'd oscillated between wanting to write a kind of page-turner—a thriller that propelled

the reader effortlessly forward—and a more ex-
plicit commentary on the limits of self-knowledge. In good moments, I knew that those two
weren't mutually exclusive; but, in my weaker
moments, I wanted to give in to that most mid-
dlebrow indulgence of *explaining.* A fragmented
fever-dream withdrawal novel would likely be
okay to read—I didn't need to think of a backstory for Calvin; he was based entirely on me,
and I had a backstory. I could emphasize surreal
aspects with a disaffected tone, a move any amateur could pull off and seem more skilled than he
was; but would the book—my novel—say what I
wanted it to say?

What did I want it to say?

Since it was written in the third person present tense, what I wanted to say didn't matter:
readers wouldn't take it seriously enough to think
beyond the page—an amateur first novel about
drugs with no insight. I struggled to consider
a Hemingway quote about icebergs, thinking,
"iceberg . . ." then remembered a tweet I'd seen
in which someone, responding to a tweet with a
relevant Hemingway quote, preemptively apolo-
gized for quoting Hemingway.

I scrolled and read the sentences, one of

which included the phrase "a handful of," and I recoiled. A handful? What was I doing? I deleted "a handful of," feeling nihilistic and aggressive; I wanted to delete the whole section; my whole novel; a handful, I thought mockingly; I looked around the kitchen mumbling, "kill myself, kill myself . . ."; I couldn't write a drug novel; I could not write a drug novel—ffff.

Perhaps this was the reason I'd been so resistant to working on my novel all morning: I hated drug literature, which—with a few exceptions— caused anyone with a modicum of awareness to cringe. It was all, in large part, half-formed sentiment and navel-gazing drivel, seeming more to have dribbled out of the author's mouth than been penned with any intent. Even the so-called great drug authors were undeniable hacks with no skill or insight into anything lasting or true. If there was any place in literature I did not want to stake my claim, it was among the explicitly drug-addicted—or worse, the recovered.

It was not a mystery why people did drugs, nor why, when they became addicted, people quit. Because of this obvious fact, which was one of the few truly uncomplicated realities of life, every book about drugs was inherently less interesting than every book that was not about drugs. Of course, I loved drug addicts and recovering addicts. It was the impulse to write that one could not trust. I did not need to *work through*, or *process*, or *convince* myself or anyone of anything; I did not want to *tell my story*; I did not need to *pat myself on the back* or *publicly lash myself* about it, as it were. I could not and did not want to help anyone either—at least not through my fiction. Drug novels, I knew, despite many deluded claims, always offered half-mystically and without evidence, did not *help*. All one had to do was look at the lives of those who claimed that this or that drug novel had helped them in this or that manner, and it became immediately clear that what they really meant was that this or that novel helped them *feel better*—for a short period of time.

And yet, I had started a drug novel; I had not only started a drug novel, but had been working on my drug novel every morning for months; I had been working on it all morning! Plus, it was in third person present tense, I thought, like having an unpleasant flashback, simultaneously accusing and defending myself. Third . . . I felt grim.

There are no . . . Fff. Th—there . . . Ffff . . .

thh. I could not think of a single book in third person present tense except mine. There are no books in third person present tense, I thought. I repeated this distractedly a few times, like a kind of mantra, until all at once the thought sounded bright, like a song, and I felt as if I were skipping through a field, or ripping something large in half on purpose. There are no other books in third person present tense! This distressing fact, which had tormented me for the months that I'd been working on my novel, was one way in which my novel's perspective and tense could actually work: it would be the only book of its kind. It was precisely because most drug novels were in the first person past tense that they were so sentimental and unseemly; third person present tense was unprecedented; it could seem intentional and literary, as opposed to pornographic and self-absorbed, like most drug novels; the intensity of the protagonist's feelings would be happening *off the page*, along with everything else, creating *an effect* . . .

What a glorious and unexpected insight. My third person present tense novel, which all morning had felt voiceless and empty and thin and rather pointless in a bad way, now felt voiceless and empty and thin and rather pointless in a good way. Since first person past tense lent itself well to narcissistic bile and sentimentality, third person present tense would resist that model, which had become so popular, and be a new frontier on the horizon of drug novels. There would be no glorification, no personality, no feeling, no justification, no texture, no insight, no anything . . . Yes . . . My thoughts began to feel like they were buzzing around in a cage, and I slammed my hands on the table on both sides of my laptop. A breakthrough. I'd worked long and hard all morning to arrive at this conclusion about my third person present tense novel, and now that I had, I could finally get to work.

I stretched my arms in front of me, palms out, fingers interlocked, then tapped my fingers gently on the keyboard, like an authority figure, pausing to deliberate. I scrolled to the end of what I'd written of my novel so far—I'd left off at a flashback of Calvin in rehab years prior to the pooping debacle—then I scrolled down farther, to near the bottom of the document, where a few unfinished fragments remained. I could edit them now, add them to the novel, then be done for the day.

I considered the first fragment, also a flash-back, in which Calvin is Gmail-chatting with Paul—a character based on Li—and rationalizing their drug use: children were prescribed Adder-all and Xanax, and in some cases opiates, to take daily; others ate junk food which, in many ways, was less healthy than drugs; Calvin listened to music every day, and while alone, which didn't mean he "had a problem" with listening to music; drugs helped him to be productive, to cope with stress and anxiety and depression; they were fun.

I could edit the arguments, I considered, to make them as compelling as possible, then jux-tapose them with the present tense action in my novel. I needed to situate them somewhere other than a flashback; flashbacks always seemed egregious and unreal. Perhaps Calvin could en-counter an email from Paul while he is lying in bed, and remember the rationale, or something; it would be good to juxtapose the rationale with Calvin's current situation; to maximally illustrate the outcome of Calvin's most *rational* thinking. I wanted to show that ideas put into practice had to map onto reality; if they didn't work, they didn't actually make sense in some fundamental way.

No—I needed to resist the expository urge,

as well as the urge to try to control what I was saying; I'd literally just decided this . . . my breakthrough . . . I reminded myself to stick with concrete action only, like I was grasping at something thin, slippery and wiggling. I looked at the stray pieces of my novel, reading sentences too quickly or too slowly, trying to formulate a plan, then opened a new tab, opened Twitter, then closed it. How could I show, through concrete action or detail, that Calvin had had every *reason* to do everything that he did? Logic always had its own internal coherence; it was the framework that logic was embedded in, and the thing it was oriented toward, that gave or did not give life to reason, I thought, in a forced, grandiose tone, perhaps trying to fake my way into a serious state of mind, or return to the self-assured tone of my *Woodcutters* novel. I opened and closed Twitter; the urge to explain things kept welling up in me; I couldn't think of what, concretely, I wanted to write about; I felt tense and bored; I wanted to delete my novel.

Li had, I recalled, told me that he was interested in reading about my experiences though, many of which were referenced in my novel. I'd at various points told him I would send him stories about things that had happened to me over the years, and then never followed through. I recalled shakily penning a few paragraphs in one of my intensive outpatient classes, which mostly just described the dirty blue jeans I'd worn without washing for weeks at a time to my factory job, where I'd stood folding boxes, putting brake calipers into the boxes, then stacking the boxes, and where I shot heroin, when I had enough, on every cigarette or lunch break. I still hadn't written about this time period either: on the day I'd overdosed, I'd gotten paid, and bought twenty Klonopin from the boss's son—the only person I'd ever earnestly used the word "brat" to describe, who everyone hated and who charged too much for his pills—which I'd incorrectly understood to be .5 milligrams each; in reality they were 2 milligrams, and after eating a fistful to quell the oncoming sickness, I immediately blacked out, forgetting that I'd taken Klonopin then taking more repeatedly throughout the day, so that when I'd gotten out of work, met up with my heroin dealer, squared my debt, and gotten a couple points to get rid of the sickness, I was on sixteen milligrams of Klonopin; the mixture made my heart stop beating.

•

"Chingaro, chingaro, shhhhhh," I whispered, approaching the bed. "Chingaro, chingaro, ching-a-ro." I sang the last bit operatically, with my arm out, palm up, moving left to right in front of me. "Chingaro" was just one of the many special words I shared with Dillon; there was a host of phrases, songs, dances, and noises that we shared; we had our own uncorrupted language. It was the purest form of communication: I talked and he couldn't understand me or respond, unless it was one of three commands. I was never more myself than when I was talking or singing to Dillon. I climbed onto the bed and rubbed my hands in his fur, stroking his torso and patting his back; he panted and looked up at me, wagging his tail.

"Don't wake your mamka," I said, loudly enough to wake Violet, who grinned sleepily. I leaned over her and kissed her forehead, warm and somewhat moist with sleep. "I'm taking Dillon to the woods," I whispered, then pecked her again.

Violet shifted, slowly writhed, then emitted a high-pitched yelp-yawn combination, stretching her arms up and over her head. She covered her mouth with her hand and said, "Okay," pulling the covers tight around her shoulders. She turned away from me.

My face hovered over her face and kissed it five times quickly. Violet wiggled, then turned onto her back and opened her eyes, rolling them around in their sockets. "What time is it?" she breathed.

"Two-thirty," I said. "Just kidding, ten-thirty-ish." I kissed her face until she pushed me away and said, "Stop," half-smiling. I made a pouty face even though her eyes were closed. "But, but, I love you."

"I l'ew," she mumbled. "I l'ew."

"I love you," I said in a breathy staccato; I kissed her on the neck, then bent over even farther and wrapped my arms around her and squeezed.

She patted my back and kind of groaned— "Okay." She grinned in a way that meant "leave me alone."

I pecked at her cheek four times, paused, then pecked another seven; I felt overcome with the desire to smother her. "Okay," I said, "I'll go." I turned to Dillon, who was lying on his stomach with his back legs splayed out behind him like a frog. "But first," I said, in a tone like a magician— the coffee had made itself felt now, I wanted to giggle—and then couldn't think of a way to finish the bit. "Bunty," I said, addressing the dog. "Bunty, bunty."

I patted his torso three times, then motioned with my hand for him to come. He got up in a rush of excitement, then sat on Violet, confused, though still wagging. Violet wiggled. Dillon likely suspected that I was planning to trick him and shut him out of the room, something I did when Violet and I wanted to have sex. Dillon's tail swished on the covers, reminding me of a pair of pants I had when I played basketball in middle school, which made a similar sound when I walked; they had buttons up the side, and after warmups I would rip them off theatrically. Vague images of some of the kids I played basketball with floated phantasmically in my imagination—I couldn't see them, in some sense, as I was staring now with unfocused eyes at Dillon, but sub-visually, in something like pre-image images, they were there: my friend Chris, a star athlete, a jar of peanut butter and his dog; Keith's red puffy face; my coach's white hair and gut; my swishy pants—then nothing. "Come on," I whispered to Dillon, "we're going to the woods."

I coaxed Dillon into the living room, where he

began marching in circles and rubbing up against my legs like a cat, though less gracefully. I walked through the kitchen to the back door and opened it; I felt a slight breeze as I stood there. Dillon ran outside; I closed the door.

In the kitchen, I filled a glass with water, chugged it, then placed it in the dish-filled sink. The dirty dishes distressed me. Violet would probably wake while I was gone, come into the kitchen for breakfast, and see the pile of dirty dishes; the first thing she would encounter in her day would be a pile of dirty dishes and it would be my fault; I knew how dirty dishes—and dirtiness in general—stressed her out; I felt distantly distressed, considering her potential future distress, but also acutely distressed, as over time I'd come to dislike dirty dishes too. I stood there, over the sink, leaning on the counter, wondering how I could get away with not doing the dishes, or if doing only some of the dishes would make it seem less like an egregious pile of dishes and more like a few dishes in the sink.

I'd first heard of the concept of mindfulness in the context of washing dishes. My therapist at the time had used dishwashing as an example of it—"Notice how the water and soap feel on your hand, how the glass or the plastic or silverware feels and sounds, how the soap smells"—and I'd associated meditation with dishwashing ever since. I didn't like to do either; but, remembering this while imagining Violet's imminent encounter with the dishes, combined with the intensity of the caffeine and a growing insecurity about how my sink was always full of dirty dishes, I decided to do what needed to be done.

I washed the plates first. Plates were harder to fit on the dish rack than other dishes, which is why they had allotted slots; they were difficult to stack any which way, unlike mugs, cups, and bowls, which you could arrange in endless variations on top of and next to each other quite painlessly. I rubbed each plate with a soapy sponge in a circular motion, rinsed it beneath the running water, then slipped it into the allotted slots on the dish rack; I instantly felt more at ease. Placing the plates in the thin slots on the dish rack reminded me of the satisfied feeling I got the first time I found a mug that fit in the cupholder in my car (I hadn't expected it to fit, then it slipped snugly in, surprising me), or the first time I learned I could conceal a pill bottle in a film container.

At the beginning of consciousness, space was

undifferentiated, so people created, or discerned, *sacred* spaces and objects—like tops of mountains and stacked rocks—to orient themselves in the world. The feeling I got from slipping plates into their allotted slots on the dish rack was the present manifestation of such need to differentiate space, I half-considered, already feeling, apparently, the effects of *meditation*; the satisfaction stretched all the way back to the beginning of consciousness; it pleased me without my having to think about it. Cleanliness . . . is next to . . . I thought noncommittally.

I finished with the plates and moved on to the few mugs, which I stacked haphazardly between the plates and the edge of the dish rack, a balancing act that was also satisfying, but more effortfully so; I stacked some bowls there as well, then started on the silverware.

"Washing dishes makes me feel good," I recalled my dad having said once as he washed my dishes, which had been piled high, during the time in my life that my novel was based on. My parents had come to pick me up because my benzodiazepine withdrawal was so severe and my soon-to-be-ex-girlfriend was scared. My father had filled one side of the sink with soapy water and one side of the sink with clean water, and had placed the dish rack on the counter, on a towel, next to the sink; he'd rubbed the dirty dishes in the soapy water, dunked them in the clean water, rubbed them again, then placed them in the dish rack. This was also the method my then girlfriend had used. My dad did it because it was efficient; my then girlfriend to conserve water.

I didn't use that method because it didn't feel as satisfying. I liked watching the yellow gunk from an egg crusted onto an old plate or some crumbs from a sandwich slide off and down into the sink while getting blasted with the faucet water; feeling the powerful flow of the faucet, as opposed to the swamp-like murk of the dirty, soapy, still water. Standing water carried deadly bacteria; running water sustained life. I considered how my ancestors, thousands of years ago, must have felt upon finding running water in the wild. Some small part of me must have felt that now.

Standing at the kitchen sink washing silverware, I drifted between satisfying ancestral fantasy, more recent memory, attempts at mindful awareness of the texture of the dishes, soap, and water, and a dim awareness of my novel, until the dish rack was filled up.

The back door creaked as Dillon nudged it open with his snout, then hurtled past me into the living room. He pounced on a bone, stretched in the downward dog position, and wiggled his bottom half vigorously.

"Bunty monty," I said. "Bunty monty, bunty moonda." He ran to me and jumped up, then stood panting. I rubbed his torso. "Yes," I said ominously; then, cheerfully, "Yes yes." I began to dance a little, singing one of our favorite songs: a classic nineties hip-hop-style number that went "Bunty, bunty chanstadontay / pisto pasto chanstadontay." Dillon began panting more frantically and running around. "Youwan go? Youwan go woods?" Dillon panted deliriously; I slapped his compact body, then went and closed the back door; Dillon ran toward his leash, hanging from a hook on the wall next to the front door, and nudged it.

I felt like I was in a simulation of the forest, suddenly submerged in trees and dirt, my eyes kind of unfocused and wet due to the wind. The leaves had started to turn; there were classically autumnal colors all around me; red, orange, yellow;

brown tree trunks; green grass; the sand-like trail on which we walked. A haze seemed to hang over everything, but the sun was shining strong.

There were many spindly trees, some shorter than me, sticking up out of the ground; some shot into the sky, thick-trunked and looming. I'd once seen a tree fall in these woods; it had creaked, as they often do in the wind, but this time split, crashed down, then landed in between the branch and trunk of a shorter tree below it.

We approached a downward slope, at the bottom of which was a bridge, then a hill back up; I considered whether or not it was a valley, thinking, Valley . . . ? then, "As I walk through the valley of the shadow of death"—the inaugural line of "Gangsta's Paradise" by Coolio—a song I hadn't thought about in years, and which I'd learned of via Weird Al Yankovic's parody, "Amish Paradise," as a child. Seeing only the general outlines and shapes of things through my second face, which was usually reserved for scrolling, I recalled that now had not been the first time I'd thought-sung "Gangsta's Paradise" at this exact spot on the trail; perhaps this time I had really only remembered having thought it in the past, the inaugural line occurring angularly, and not directly, as I mistakenly thought I had experienced it.

I shook my head, bringing the colors and the varied shapes around me into focus; I scanned the far distance for people, and, seeing none, unleashed Dillon. He sprinted away, a short burst, then stopped to smell a plant; I strolled leisurely past him and then, as he took his time sniffing, beckoned him impatiently.

"Dillon," I said, in a high-pitched tone. I jumped into a half-squat and slapped my thighs, rather suddenly; he stayed sniffing. "Dillon," I said, making a move toward him.

Dillon had become so attuned to me calling his name whenever there was something potentially enticing nearby—passerby, deer, squirrel— that he had learned to check around him before coming, just in case. Looking around now, knowing I'd moved toward him, and in anticipation of a potential succulent woodland offering, he pantingly scanned the woods in all directions except mine—then he hurtled toward me. He passed me and went partway up the hill; I walked with my hands in my pockets behind him.

My legs strained walking up the steep incline; I felt grateful to be walking with my dog.

Sometimes, as now, when I walked with my hands in my pockets, I imagined myself being seen by another and perceived myself as looking like a lumberjack, confidently taking my time, moving at an unhurried but masculine pace, with my dog, hands in pockets, in the woods. This was how I'd imagined myself during therapy.

When my most recent therapist had asked me to describe to her my "happy place"—an impossibly old-fashioned suggestion which I'd initially thought was a joke—I froze; I couldn't imagine anywhere that wasn't my house or the therapist's office. I told her that I couldn't think of anywhere; she told me that it was okay, to just sit and wait for my happy place to reveal itself, but after five minutes of sitting in what for me became a panic-stricken silence, it was clear that no happy place would emerge. I'd come to therapy, I had thought, for help with my anxiety—instead, I was about to have a panic attack.

The therapist asked gently, "What about a favorite place to go? It doesn't have to be real. Maybe think of somewhere warm? Or a castle? It can be anything."

A castle? I'd thought disbelievingly; I'd felt like I was being tortured. This must be what it was like to get tortured, I'd thought then, sitting in her dim office, in the basement of her home.

"Do you like water, or snow, or nature—"

"The woods," I'd said, relieved.

She'd asked me to describe specific aspects of the woods, which for the most part I'd been unable to do. "I thought you were a writer," she'd joked— an unoriginal jab—and I told her that the most accurate description of what the woods smelled like was *the woods* and that the trees looked *like trees*, but she wasn't impressed, and mistook, it had seemed, my earnestness for sardonic aggression.

I mentally replayed a fragmented version of our conversation as I leisurely strolled through the woods with Dillon—*my happy place*—now.

"It's . . . grey," I'd said when she'd asked me what the weather was like. I liked going to the woods when it was grey or raining, because it all but guaranteed no one would be there. The therapist seemed not to understand that either; in retrospect she didn't understand anything at all. The remainder of our sessions had begun with guided meditation: first I would tense then release specific parts of my body, on her command; then she would describe to me my happy place.

You are walking in the woods. It is grey and

lightly drizzling. Dillon is running around; he is sniffing a plant. You are wearing a comfortable hoodie, and drinking a hot cup of coffee. There is no one around . . .

Now, the sun cast pixelated patterns over everything. There was a slight breeze, not quite cold, but occasionally a strong gust bit my eyes. I hated that therapist; I suddenly remembered a tweet that read "I like my weather like I like my music: late fifties, early sixties," which perturbed me—I was supposed to be taking in nature, not thinking about my old therapist, or Twitter.

I tried to focus on the beauty around me, but felt too self-conscious to earnestly experience anything. I closed my eyes and tried what my new therapist called *diaphragmatic breathing*, feeling my belly extend and contract, counting my breaths in and out as I walked. When I opened my eyes, the colors were richer, deeper; for a moment, I felt thoughtless and free.

I looked around. Dillon ran after a squirrel, jumping over a fallen tree trunk in pursuit.

Bunty gazelle, I thought wistfully. I wanted to film him for my Instagram story; I patted my pockets, forgetting I had intentionally left my phone in the car; I felt inside my hoodie pocket too.

Wind swept through the woods; the trees swayed. I felt as though I was watching a movie; unable, again, to absorb my surroundings in any meaningful sense; things seemed seen through a screen; I marched along, trying to focus on that which surrounded me—there were beautiful, complex systems operating outside of my control, that had nothing to do with me or what I wanted, that I wasn't in control of and that were ultimately good; I knew the bad things I was capable of, the kinds of things that gripped and then possessed a person—I'd worked all morning on a novel about the outcome of that—and so, walking in the woods, I conceived of myself as surrounded by whatever the opposite of that was, then abstracted that out, distilled it one hundred times into purity; I was cognizant of a *goodest good*; goodness itself; and I consciously oriented myself toward it.

The leaves rustled above me; I saw a hawk circling. I breathed and closed my eyes. My face felt warm, the sun sedating; spots of light zoomed bouncily like angry bees behind my eyelids. I breathed deeply again and felt grateful: for Dillon; for Violet; for my life, which was organized such that I'd been able to work on my novel all morning then come to the woods on a whim. I felt grateful to have left my phone in the car. A cloud moved in front of the sun and I opened my eyes, feeling, in the decisecond it took for me to open them, self-conscious of the fact that I'd just experienced something stereotypically hippie-like.

I looked in front of and behind me, but couldn't see Dillon.

I squinted and looked into the distance, scanning the woods. "Dillon!" I yelled. My eyes were still adjusting to the light. "Dill!" I put my hand above my eyes like a visor. Had Dillon seen another walker and run up to them? "Dillon!" I saw a tiny speck in the distance—a tree stump. I scanned the woods dizzyingly and felt momentarily nauseated: everything looked like Dillon.

"Dill!" I yelled again. If I'd had my phone with me I would've been filming him, I considered, not closing my eyes and letting him run off and disappear. There was nothing I could do, and somehow I wasn't worried.

I assumed a leisurely posture.

My thoughts alternated between shit-talking my novel, quasi visualizations of the internet, anxious anticipation of unforeseen passersby, and negative feelings about my life in general.

My brain felt glitchy, like a malfunctioning computer; my thoughts were like unwanted pop-ups. If technology strove to eventually emulate consciousness, the engineers had already unwittingly accomplished it: shitty pop-ups and unwanted emails were exactly like my thoughts.

I moved my hand toward my pocket, like a reflex, to make a note about my thoughts being like pop-ups, then remembered that I didn't have my phone. It occurred to me that I could include some of these kinds of thoughts in my *Woodcutters* novel; I subconsciously patted my pockets again for my phone.

I narrated the pop-up thing to myself a few times to try to remember it, mumbling, "Pop-up . . . consciousness . . . pop-up . . ." while the sun hit my face and hands. It seemed hard to write a novel. Thomas Bernhard was a genius, with a profound understanding of things; I was only just now beginning, perhaps, perhaps not, to see . . .

As I walked on the path, I considered the rest of my day. Should I keep trying to work on my novel? Or my *Woodcutters* novel? Both prospects seemed bleak. It appeared as though I could either write a bad novel from a distressing point of view and in a distressing tense, about a hackneyed topic; or further alienate my peers by writing a *Woodcutters*-style novel that would solidify my unfavorable position in life, and likely not end up like *Woodcutters* at all. I was not smart enough to write the kinds of books I wanted to write; it was entirely possible that no matter which novel I worked on it would never come out anyway. Then again, I felt confident that some independent press would put it out; independent presses put out anything now; there were a million of them and they all, more or less, put out anything. I nobly resolved to be fine with this.

What had initially felt like a purposeful endeavor, my *Woodcutters* novel, now felt like a misguided, reactionary attempt to lash out. Maybe I could work on it slowly, over a period of years, as my worldview progressed, and it could turn into something great, I quixotically considered, not really believing myself. I felt a twinge of defensive hatred toward Eric; if I waited, maybe I wouldn't want to write it at all. It was, after all, just a novel. The fact of its being fiction would grant me the freedom to be wrong. As long as it was written well . . .

At the very least it would be good to work on,

to clarify my thoughts and feelings, if only to myself. At best it would be a huge success. I considered the rest of my day.

Maybe I should spend time with Violet? We could work together at a coffee shop or library or go somewhere she wanted to go; perhaps today would be a good day for a date. I wondered what Violet would think of my novels. The weather was perfect; I suspected any further attempts to work on writing would almost certainly result in more unproductive stress. But I also felt energized thinking about writing my new novel; I had momentum and direction. Maybe it didn't need to be exactly like *Woodcutters*, but some combination of *Woodcutters* and thoughts like the one I'd just had about pop-ups and consciousness; instead of sitting in a wing chair at an *artistic dinner*, the protagonist could be sitting in front of his laptop, looking at social media.

I didn't need to work on it any more today; it seemed like it might sustain my interest; it would be a good excuse to abandon my hellish third person present tense novel . . .

I considered my future as an infamous novelist as I walked alongside Dillon in the woods. It would take a lot of work. I tried to mentally construct a to-do list for the rest of the day. Gym . . . I thought. G . . . I distractedly surveyed the woods for passersby; I thought I'd heard leaves crunching in the distance; they were just the leaves beneath my boots.

I continued on the path then turned around.

ACKNOWLEDGMENTS

Thank you to my wife, Nicolette Polek, for your help with this book and for willing the good.

To my brilliant editor Kendall Storey, and everyone at Soft Skull Press.

To my family; Tao Lin and Yuka Igarashi of the Burnt Meadow Residency; Kevin Hascher, Michael W. Clune, Scott McClanahan, Megan Boyle, Zachary Schwartz, Andrew Weatherhead, Alex Mussawir, Adam Humphreys, Chris Clemans, and Giancarlo DiTrapano.

JORDAN CASTRO is the author of two poetry books and the former editor of *New York Tyrant Magazine*. He is from Cleveland, Ohio. *The Novelist* is his first novel.